A HANDFUL OF STARS

A Novel By
Daniel W. Weeks

PublishAmerica
Baltimore

© 2010 by Daniel W. Weeks.
All rights reserved. No part of this book may be reproduced, stored in a retrieval system or transmitted in any form or by any means without the prior written permission of the publishers, except by a reviewer who may quote brief passages in a review to be printed in a newspaper, magazine or journal.

First printing

This is a work of fiction. Names, characters, places, and incidents either are the product of the author's imagination or are used fictitiously. Any resemblance to actual persons, living or dead, events, or locales is entirely coincidental.

PublishAmerica has allowed this work to remain exactly as the author intended, verbatim, without editorial input.

Hardcover 978-1-4512-0520-6
Softcover 978-1-4512-0504-6
PAperback 978-1-4512-4661-2
PUBLISHED BY PUBLISHAMERICA, LLLP
www.publishamerica.com
Baltimore

Printed in the United States of America

ACKNOWLEDGMENTS

I wish to express my gratitude to all the members of The Creative Writing Circle at Heritage Senior Center in Irving, Texas for the encouragement and suggestions they gave me during the writing process of, "A Handful of Stars."

I especially want to think Pat Davenport, Judy McGonagill, Al Cavaness, and Candice Lee for their proofreading efforts on my behalf.

Last, but not least, I want to think my loving wife Emily for her forbearance of my crankiness during the writing process, and for her assistance with the research.

Many of the titles that appear in the Bibliography are books she bought for me for my enjoyment and for research.

Table of Contents

CHAPTER 1 9
The Trip to Texas

CHAPTER 2 29
Clear Fork Station

CHAPTER 3 49
A Handful of Stars

CHAPTER 4 57
Bad Men, Bad Indians, and Four good Women

CHAPTER 5 109
The Civil War Years

CHAPTER 6 127
A Handful Of Stars

EPILOGUE 137

BIBLIOGRAPHICAL NOTE 139

FOOTNOTES 141

A HANDFUL OF STARS

CHAPTER 1

The Trip to Texas

"Look alive there boys," Captain Jacobs snarled. "Put a little grunt into that poling. You wanta get there today, don't you?"

He could see the docks at St Louis far down the muddy river from where he endlessly poled the keelboat, seeming to get no closer than it had been hours before.

I have to write a letter to Sis when I get to St Louis (Sis; Theophilus' baby sister who could never pronounce his name when she was small, so he became simply Tee). *Its been more than a year since I wrote the last one.*

Tee began to regret his decision to hire on to pole the keelboat up the Missouri River three days after the boat pulled out of St. Louis almost a year ago.

The work was mind numbingly boring, and back-breakingly tedious.

Stand at the prow of the boat, on either side, lodge the pole into the river bottom and heave with all your might to move the boat forward into the current. Shuffle your way to the stern, heaving all the while, pull the pole out of the mud and return to the prow to do it all over again, hour after hour, day after day.

He was tempted to jump off the stern, swim ashore, and go home.

He would have done it except for the fact that he had persuaded his younger brother Jim to join him in this adventure, and the fact that when a man did jump ship Captain Jacobs shot him in the head and left his body for the turtles and snakes to dispose of.

"The rest of you dogs beware, desertion of my ship is a capital offence," the captain growled, holding his pistol leveled on the crew, daring any man to try him.

◇

When the keelboat finally came near the docks, men were ready to toss ropes over the mooring post to make the boat secure.

A wisp of wind off the shore brought the smells of men, Black, White, Chinese, Indian, Creoles, burley Irishmen, and mules and oxen all sweating and working to load boats and unload other boats. The smell of the men, the animals, manure, urine, and dead fish all blended into a cornucopia of men shouting orders, men cursing and arguing, bull-whackers cracking their whips, and other men singing mournful work songs to set the pace of their work.

"Stay aboard," the captain ordered, "till I come back with your pay."

"Why don't we go with you?" someone asked.

"Because I say so," the captain snarled, squaring himself into a fighting stance, touching his right hand to the butt of the pistol he'd shot the deserter with, he stared the men into submission. "I ain't ever cheated a man out of his pay yet. I'll be back in an hour, so just set tight."

"You ain't back in one hour, you'll be in hell in two," the surly Indian everyone called Chief simply because he was the only Indian on the boat grumbled under his breath.

A HANDFUL OF STARS

George Miller, Dirty George, so called by the crew for his lack of hygiene, was a wiry little man who didn't possess great brut strength but had phenomenal stamina said calmly, "I've sailed with him before. He'll be back."

◇

Theophilus Wells stood six feet tall with strong arms and a barrel chest giving him a shape that was somehow reminiscent of a bulldog, but his facial features weren't consistent with that image for his face was narrow with high cheekbones a thin nose, thin lips, and steel gray eyes that some saw as cold.

He wasn't a gregarious man, but neither was he cold. Perhaps some people saw the remains of a heart that was broken eight years ago when Lela chose to marry Charlie Haskell instead of marrying Tee.

He promised Lela he would honor her decision, but his heart had never been party to the promise. Since that day, he had drifted around the Mississippi and Missouri River country doing whatever odd job came along.

Jin is a carbon copy of Tee, but an inch shorter, with brown eyes wore a short-cropped mustache that he thought disguised his slightly misshapen upper lip.

Tee sat on the boat deck leaning his back against the wall of the deckhouse watching the men on the docks doing their work. Their skin glistening with sweat, they all wore slouchy dirty cloths with their shirts of all colors sweated through, and hats of every description.

The river flowed under the boat and swirled off the prow in lazy eddies on its way to the sea. The men on the dock swirled in lazy eddies doing their work. The noise, the motion, the smells of it all left Tee feeling jangled, and longing for the solitude of the prairie.

Tee and Jim had talked of becoming partners in some business venture or another on their return to St Louis. He considered it the wishful thinking of tired lonely men who were trapped on the keelboat as surely as if they were locked in a prison. It was the talk of desperate men longing to stand on a higher rung of the ladder.

Tee's thought drifted with the river current, down the river to Cairo, Illinois where he knew Lela was and to the memory of her that haunted him as strongly as it ever had.

She stood five-feet-five, a lovely eighteen-year-old. Her long blond hair hung in ringlets about her slender neck. Her cheeks were round, somehow reminiscent of apples, leaving Tee with the perpetual urge to nibble.

When she wore a dress that exposed her upper arms and shoulders above her round breast who's curve matched that of her apple like cheeks, the effect was intoxicating.

Her twenty-five inch waist above her perfect hips, with an occasional glimpse of a trim ankle atop a graceful foot was devastating.

They sat on a blanket that was spread under a large oak tree within sight of the river on a sunny afternoon in the summer of 1850.

"And where are you supposed to be this afternoon Miss Atkins?" he asked eventually.

"I'm visiting Ruth."

"That's a little dangerous, isn't it? Your father knows her and her family well."

"It'll all be out in the open when you ask father for my hand," she cooed.

"What do you think the odds are that he'll shoot me before he agrees to our marriage?" he asked, only half teasing.

"Oh he hates you because he hates your father. That's certainly true enough."

"And my father hates him," he added. "All over a disagreement concerning a twenty dollar horse fifteen years ago. It's hard to imagine two intelligent gentlemen being such peevish old men."

"Father is dead-set that I'm going to marry Charlie Haskell."

"You've known Charlie all your life. Do you love him?"

"Yes. I want to marry both of you."

"Ha, maybe I should look elsewhere for a bride in that case," he teased.

"Maybe you should if you're afraid to ask father for my hand," she smiled; both of them knowing that neither of them meant any of this last exchange.

After a moments silence he looked at her mischievously saying, "I know what we should do. When I see your father we should confide that you're pregnant."

Her eyes were angry, her voice shrill, "Theophilus Wells that is not funny. You know a girl has nothing but her reputation. The slightest whisper of that would ruin me for life. Don't you dare even tease about that!"

"Don't tease me about your loving Charlie Haskell."

A light breeze rustled the leaves of the oak tree they sat under causing dappling shafts of sunlight to ripple over them, cooling their ardor.

After a few moments of silence, she asked evenly," Will you see father tonight?"

He took her hand in his and kissing it gently answered, "Yes, I will."

◇

When Tee called at the Atkins home that evening Lela made certain that it was she who answered his knock on the door.

The couple walked arm-in-arm into the study where her father was seated reading a newspaper.

"Father, Mr. Wells is calling," she crooned.

"What the hell does he want?" Looking up from his paper,

"Oh! It's the young Mr. Wells. What the hell do you want?"

"Sir, I pray you will allow me the honor of your daughters hand in marriage,' he said earnestly.

Lela's heart jumped with joy when her father rose and stalked to them, she assuming him coming to congratulate them.

Her joy was dashed when he reached them and slapped Tee across the face, snarling angrily, "The Oaks at daybreak."

"No!" she shrieked. "No God no. I wont have you two kill each other over me. Tee say no, don't accept his challenge. Father, withdraw, apologize!"

After a long moment, Tee swallowed his anger, and announced sternly, "Sir, for Lela's sake I decline your challenge. But, both of you know this, if you ever call me again I'll kill you."

Tee turned on his heels and stomped angrily out of the house.

◇

The next day Tee saw Ruth and persuaded her to take a letter to Lela setting a clandestine meeting with her.

Tee waited under the oak where the dappling sun had soothed them only two days before.

He waited long past the appointed hour. When he was about to despair of the enterprise, she came.

He tried to hold her in his arms, but she refused.

"Lela I want you to come away with me. We'll be married in the first town we come to, and then we'll go on to California. They're digging up gold in chunks out there, and we'll be rich in no time."

She replied sadly, "No, I can't."

"Why?"

"I'm going to marry Charlie."

"I won't stand for it."

"Tee, promise me you won't make trouble."

"I promise you I'll raise hell and put a prop under it."

"It's decided. There's no undoing it." She begged, "If you love me, promise me you won't make trouble."

Seeing the pain in her, he melted before her saying, "All right Lela, we'll have it your way."

Looking away he continued, "I'll quit this country for if I don't I'll never be able to keep that pledge. Sooner than later I'd get around to killing your Father, or Charlie, or both of 'em"

Touching two fingers of his right hand to his lips and then to hers, he said softly, "I wish you well. I wish you happiness. My sister will know where to find me if you ever want me."

With those words, he took his leave of her.

◇

The Captain was back in an hour and paid the men as promised.

Tee and Jim were already on the dock when the Captain called after them, "You men be back here in a week. We sail for Dakota Territory in a week."

"Yes'er Captain," Tee replied, *like hell I will.*

"Now then, Jim, where's that rooming house you've been telling me about since we left here?" Tee asked.

"It's up the hill yonder," Jim answered pointing a little to their left. "I know you'll like it. It's run by a big German woman who cooks the best yeast roles you ever tasted, and she keeps everything as clean as a pin too."

"I want a good bath, a good meal, and a soft bed that ain't moving, and I hope she has a room that looks out away from the river. If I don't never see that miserable Missouri River again it'll be too damned soon," Tee asserted.

Jim led the way along a muddy rough street leading away

from the docks. The street was lined with dingy dives that catered to the men who worked the river and the docks.

"I wouldn't mind picking up a jug," Jim offered.

Tee agreed, "Now there's good idea. A very good idea. Yes'er, a very good idea!"

◇

Mrs. Fickle's Boarding House had, in years past, been a fine home in the upper-crust part of town, but now its paint was peeling and the trim was sagging here and there. It generally reflected the decline of the neighborhood.

Jim assured Tee the house was kept clean and the food was great, and the price was agreeable.

There was a well-worn parlor and a large dining room on the first floor. On the second floor several room partitions had been removed in order to make a large barracks like room where cots lined the walls, each cot being furnished with a footlocker.

Tee was grateful that he drew a cot that sat under a window that faced south from which he couldn't see the river unless he leaned over just so. South was the most likely direction for a breeze, and the notion of a soft breeze struck Tee as most agreeable.

By the time Tee and Jim stowed their belongings in their footlockers enough damage had been done to the jug that Tee didn't really care much about the amenities of Mrs. Fickle's establishment.

Now he wanted a bath.

The bathhouse was a picket building constructed of rough sawed planks with a low shed roof in back of the main house. It was equipped with round wooden tubs in which the men knelt to bathe themselves in warm water that was carried in by the bucketful by a black teenage boy.

A, "first tub," that is a tub of clean water that no one had bathed in before you, cost an extra dime. A dry towel, not necessarily fresh, a washcloth, not necessarily fresh, and a pan of water for shaving were included at no extra charge.

The black teenager's mother was the laundress for Mrs. Fickle and would wash and rough dry the boarder's clothes for 25 cents per #3 tub[1] full of dry clothes.

◇

Having finished their bath and shave, Tee and Jim settle themselves on the front porch where the smell of Mrs. Fickle's cooking, especially the smell of the yeast rolls, whetted their appetites almost beyond endurance.

They barely had time to manage a quick pull on the jug before Mrs. Fickle called the boarders to dinner.

That evening the dinner consisted of fried pork chops, turnips cooked in their own greens, dried pinto beans, and deep-dish apple pie.

And, oh yes, yeast rolls with butter and honey.

◇

After dinner Tee and Jim sat on the porch watching the gathering darkness.

Jim loaded his pipe and lit it with a Lucifer[2]* he'd drawn from his pocket.

Tee light a cigarillo and took a long deep draw, blowing a cloud of smoke into the twilight.

"I never could get the hang of keeping a pipe going," Tee commented idly. "I always had the bowl so hot I couldn't hold it or the damned thing was stone cold."

"It took me a long time to learn to keep it going smooth," Jim replied. "You have to clear your mind of just about everything else and pay strict attention to the pipe. That's why I like it I guess.

"Even now if I let my mind wonder too much it'll go out on me."

Jim took a drag on his pipe, and letting the smoke out of his mouth as he spoke, said, "I's talking to a gent I sat by at dinner who told me that John Butterfield[3] is hiring people to operate stagecoach relay stations out west, and we could probably get one if we want to.

"Does that sound like anything you would want to get into?" Jim asked.

Tee thought for a moment and answered, "Yeah. I sure am tired of this river work. Some wide-open country sounds good.

"If we get it, maybe we can sell food and drink to the passengers and make a little on the side."

"Well then, we'll go see Butterfield tomorrow," Jim said.

After a few moments of silence Tee commented, "You were right about this boarding house. It is a pretty good place, but it is lacking in one desirable amenity."

"What do you mean by that?" Jim asked, a little surprised.

"There ain't any women here."

"Oh. The sporting district is back down toward the docks," Jim replied.

"You of a mind to take a stroll?"

"Soon as I have another draw on this jug."

◇

The keelboat was drifting down the river, spinning out of control. It turned round and round, like a merry-go-round.

Oh, ga'damn, I'm so sick, Why don't someone tie this damned boat up before Caption Jacobs starts raising hell?

Tee opened his eyes only to have the rising sun shining in his face send an explosion of pain through his already bloated, aching head.

This don't look like a keelboat. This looks like an alley. Where the hell am I? What am I doing here?

Realizing that he was cold through and through, and so sick that even his hair hurt, Tee drew his knees up into his chest and hugged them.

"Tee."

He didn't respond.

"Tee. Wake up Tee."

"Leave me alone," Tee groaned. "I'm sicker that a fat dog."

"Tee, wake up. We gotta get cleaned up and go see Butterfield today."

"I don't want to see no Butterfield. I want a little hair of the dog."

"Ah come on Tee, you promised you'd go."

"I'm too sick. It would feel good to die."

"You're not gonna die of whisky poisoning, but if you don't get up I may kill you myself."

Tee looked at the man who was urging him to get up and thought he looked familiar.

Squinting, and concentrating as best he could, he finally recognized Jim.

"Here, have a slug of this," Jim said handing Tee a flask. "It'll cure what ails you."

Tee took a long drink from the flask half expecting it to bounce right back up, but it didn't.

"Now come on," Jim urged. "Lets get cleaned up and go see Butterfield."

"I don't give a hoot in hell about seeing some damned Butterfield. What in hell is it anyway?"

"John Butterfield. He's got the overland mail contract and he's hiring people to run stagecoach relay stations all the way from St Louis to San Francisco.

"You promised me we would see him and go out west somewhere and put in a station where we could make some money and maybe sell food and drink to the passengers.

"They's only gonna be two stagecoaches a week, so we'd have plenty of time to hunt and fish and do whatever we want to do," Jim asserted.

All this business about stagecoaches, and mail, and relay stations, seemed vaguely familiar to Tee, but it was all incoherent through the fog in his mind.

Tee couldn't remember the proposition of running a stagecoach relay station, but some sixth sense told him Jim was telling him the truth, so he pushed to his feet and the two of them staggered off toward Mrs. Fickle's boarding house.

◇

In the afternoon Tee and Jim made their way to the Mercantile Bank Building where John Butterfield's Overland Mail Company was headquartered on the third floor.

Upon entering the office they were greeted by a pale skinny man in a business suit that was too large for him who offered a sneering invitation for them to have a seat while he told Mr. Butterfield they were there. He strongly inferred that Butterfield wouldn't see them without an appointment.

When he returned in a couple of minutes, he said with all the condescension he could muster, "You may go in."

John Butterfield, a man in his late fifties with white hair combed flat over his head and curling a little above his ears had a round face dominated by bushy black eyebrows. A neckerchief tied around his neck partly under the collar of his shirt left him looking as if he had no neck.

Butterfield started driving stagecoaches in Up-State New York when he was nineteen years old and had the look of a man accustomed to outdoor work and exuded an air of self-confidence and physical toughness.

His speech was strongly influenced by the accent that was common in the local of his upbringing.

Butterfield, who was seated behind a large desk with his back to a window that overlooked the street, waved for Tee and Jim to be seated, and as he did so asked, "What can I do for you men?"

"We heard you're hiring men to operate relay stations for your stagecoach outfit, and we want to get in on it," Jim replied.

"I've just about hired all I need, but there is one station open out in Texas.

"It's about thirty miles south of Fort Belknap located on the Clear Fork of the Brazos River," Butterfield offered.

"Well, I guess that's as good as any," Tee observed.

"No, it isn't," Butterfield, replied. "There's nothing there but a bare gravel hill in a semi-desert region. There's not a tree in a hundred miles, and you'll have to build your own housing, feed sheds, corrals, and stock shelter, but that's what's open if you want it."

"Can we sell food and drink to the passengers on the stagecoaches?" Jim asked.

Butterfield answered, "As far as I'm concerned you can, so long as you have the teams ready to exchange when the coach pulls in. We have to make the run from St Louis to San Francisco in twenty-five days, so the coaches will have to run day and night seven days a week. There won't be much time for you to sell to the passengers."

Tee and Jim looked at each other and nodded their approval, "We'll try 'er a while," Jim said.

"What are your names?" Butterfield asked as he scribbled a note.

"I'm Jim, James Wells."

"Mine is Theophilus Wells, call me Tee."

"Brothers?" Butterfield asked.

"Little brother," Tee said pointing his thumb toward Jim.

Butterfield handed Jim the note saying, "Take this to Mike

O'Donnell, the superintendent down at the supply yard and he'll get you started.

"Go on down there today. You two are late getting here."

◇

On arriving at the supply yard the men were introduced to Mike O'Donnell who was the Texas Division Superintendent and the man to whom they would report.

They were immediately sent to a classroom and began instruction on matters of book-keeping, report writing, expense reporting, vouchers, procurement procedure, ticket selling, reporting of funds collected, and last, but not least, the handling of the mail.

The training finished, the next four days were spent preparing wagons for the trip to Texas.

Mike O'Donnell's party of fifty-two wagons were to travel directly to Texas and there to establish relay stations in the Texas Division. Other superintendents would lead parties, each to his own division, to establish stations therein.

The O'Donnell party consisted of about half single men and about half married men traveling with their wives and some with children.

Each station was planed to be about fifteen miles apart, depending on the availability of water.

The wagon train left St Louis via the road to Springfield on the last day of May.

Each wagon being pulled by six mules driven by a mule-skinner who rode the near wheel mule[4], and controlled the team with a single rein called a jerk-line[5*] and a whip that the mule-skinner popped or cracked within inches of the animals ears but only laid on the animals in the most extreme circumstance, using language suitable for skinning mules.

The mail would travel from St Louis to Tipton, Missouri by train where it would be put onto the stagecoaches that would then travel to Springfield, Missouri and from there on to San Francisco via the road that the wagon train would take from Springfield.

The road from St Louis to Springfield carried the wagon train through gently rolling hills where a goodly portion of the land was in cultivation and dotted with farmhouses and small villages.

Upon arriving in Springfield Mr. O'Donnell was well pleased with the progress of the wagon train, the trip thus far having been made in six days and without suffering any serious incident.

The wagon train was rolling south out of Springfield when Tee saw a sign pointing the way to Cairo, Illinois.

The thought of Cairo caused the memory of his love for Lela, and his hatred of Charlie Haskell to flash through his mind before he could steel himself against the melancholy that always accompanied any thought of Lela and Charlie.

Jim, seeing that Tee had fallen into a funk, said, "That sign showing the way to Cairo bring it all back to you, did it?"

"Yeah. I wish I'd never promised Lela I'd respect her decision," Tee replied, his head bowed, shoulders slumped.

"Water under the bridge. Put it out of your mind brother," Jim advised.

"I'd kill that ga'damned Charlie Haskell if I thought it would do me any good," Tee grumped.

"You know it wouldn't, so put that out of your mind too," Jim admonished.

From Springfield the wagon train moved on through the ever-steeping hills of southern Missouri toward Fayetteville, Arkansas, while Tee remained in a fog of depression for days.

Upon reaching Boston Mountain in the Ozarks the six mule teams were arranged into teams of eight mules. Only with the greatest effort were they able to pull the wagons over the narrow rough trail up the mountain, and with even greater care and determination did they make a safe decent off the mountain.

When all the wagons were safely across the mountain Mr. O'Donnell declared a day of rest for which all the members of the party were enormously grateful.

The day of rest wasn't entirely restful. There were repairs to make, stock to tend and herd to grazing, clothes to wash and mend, and numerous other chores to be attended.

In the late afternoon the women made a communal meal after which a Mr. Billings played a fiddle while some members of the party participated in a square-dance.

Tee sat with a group of single men who passed around a jug and made idle talk of no particular subject while some of them whittled away small sticks of wood as a means to busy their hands.

<>

The O'Donnell wagon train arrived at Fort Smith to find the town and the military post of the same name a beehive of activity.

Numerous roads and trails converged at Fort Smith, and the military base had been designated the quartermasters depot for the Military Department of the West.

This resulted in a great deal of riverboat traffic bringing goods and supplies up the Arkansas River, and the dispatching of large numbers of wagons and military patrols to the forts in the Indian Territory, Texas, and the New Mexico Territory.

To accommodate the riverboat's docking needs the Army had built a dock on the river near Bell Point. To facilitate travel into Indian Territory and to the forts that were serviced by the quartermaster at Fort Smith the Army had built a ferry that was operated by a civilian contractor.

A HANDFUL OF STARS

The ferry was made available to the public for their use when the Army had no need of it with the understanding that the Army had first priority on the use of the ferry.

The O'Donnell party resupplied in Fort Smith and crossed the Arkansas River taking many trips of the ferry to complete the crossing in ten hours and camped on the west side of the river.

At sunup the next morning the wagon train struck out along the California Road, so called because of the great number of forty-niners who traveled to California via this road. The road was known to some as the Texas Road, and in later years it came to be called The Butterfield Road. Its official name was The Thirty-Second Degree Trail because of its close adherence to the thirty-second degree of latitude.

The wagon train traveled the California Road through Indian Territory, coming eventually to Colliers Ferry on the Red River and thereby crossing into Texas.

The wagon train continued along the California Road where Mr. O'Donnell bought or rented facilities in the established towns for the use of the impending stagecoach service, and in open country he dispatched teams of his employees to establish way stations leaving them with the necessary tools and supplies to accomplish their task.

Leaving the town of Sherman the trail wandered across open prairie to the town of Jacksboro, also known as Jackass Flats, which had sprung up near a prairie where a herd of wild jackasses had made their home.

The ladies who were accompanying their husbands in the O'Donnell party were put into a state of shock by the number of saloons, gambling houses, and bordellos that made up the greater portion of the business in Jacksboro.

A suitable facility for the stagecoach operation was found near the town center and was procured for that purpose.

Having established the necessary facility in Jacksboro the wagon train moved out heading to Fort Belknap.

On the second day south of Fort Belknap, while traveling through more rugged country with sparse vegetation, the wagon train descended into a narrow valley with its center cut by a small stream.

At the point where the trail crossed the stream, ramps had been dug into its sheer banks in order to provide assess to ford the stream.

Having forded the stream, and climbed out of its valley onto a low rise in the surrounding prairie that was covered with gravely topsoil and small boulders Mike O'Donnell stopped the wagon train and called, "Tee, Jim, unload here. This is where we want your station."

"Butterfield said we'd be located on a river," Jim observed.

"Clear Fork of the Brazos River," O'Donnell said gesturing toward the stream they had just crossed.

"That little trickle wouldn't be a named creek where I come from," Jim replied.

"That's the beast water in the next hundred miles, and might near all the way to California. Yes sir, people would be mighty glad to see that much water all across this desert country," O'Donnell asserted.

"Butterfield sure was right about one thing, there ain't no trees around here, and mighty little of anything else," Tee observed.

Surveying the scene, Tee could see a series of low mesas off to the south and west, perhaps five miles away, standing a slightly darker shade of blue against the sky than the sky itself thereby yielding a craggy horizon. To the north and east the land was virtually flat with the jagged course of an occasional dry wash outlined with taller, greener, weeds, low thorny shrubs, and a scattering of sunflowers. The prairie appeared to be solidly covered with grass that stood eighteen to twenty-four inches tall as one viewed it from a stationary position. Upon closer observation you would find the grass growing in clumps and covering only about thirty percent of the gravely topsoil thereby giving testimony to the poor condition of the land.

CHAPTER 2

Clear Fork Station

Members of the wagon train party pitched-in to help Tee and Jim unload their tools and supplies, and to pitch their tents.

Before mounting his horse, O'Donnell addressed Tee and Jim. "Build a corral first, then a feed shed, and then you can build yourselves a house. You will want to dig a cistern when you get time because that river can get mighty brackish during dry spells."

O'Donnell mounted his horse and called for the wagon train to get underway.

Then turning to Tee and Jim said, "You gents may want to stand a night guard. This here country," gesturing with a sweep of his hand to indicate the surrounding area, "has two Indian reservations in it.

"There's one about eight miles up the river, and the other is about the same down the river.

"There's an Army camp up the river at the boundary of that reservation. Camp Cooper[6]. You gents might want to get acquainted with the commander up there.

"Them Indians feel like anything in this country belongs to them; especially horses and mules, and white men's scalps."

O'Donnell turned his horse putting it into motion leaving Tee and Jim standing in the sun.

"Ga-damned!" Tee exclaimed. "It ain't no wonder this was the last station left when we saw Butterfield."

"He said this wasn't the best location, but he sure didn't explain things," Jim observed.

Tee and Jim stood watching the wagon train trundle away, each wondering, "what next?"

After a few minutes Jim offered, "I reckon there may be some fish in that little-ol stream down yonder, so why don't we go see if we can catch us a mess for supper? We can start building a corral tomorrow."

The men cut willow branches about ten feet long and stripping them of their leaves and twigs tied fishing line onto each of them, equipped each with a hook and a cork saved from a whisky jug. They caught grasshoppers and threaded them onto the hooks. Then, funding themselves a comfortable place to sit on the riverbank they cast the lines into the water.

After a few minutes of no action, each man lit himself a smoke and patiently pretended to watch his cork.

When a little more than half an hour had passed Jim commented, "I recon these fish in this river don't like grasshoppers."

"Seems like," Tee replied dryly.

After a few more minutes Jin mused, "You know, there was some gents back home told me that they caught catfish by feeling their way along up under them overhanging banks in little-ol streams like this one."

Tee gave Jim a disapproving look.

Jim, ignoring Tee's disapproval, went on, "I don't recon it would hurt to try it, since we ain't catching nothing anyway."

"Did them gents that told you that have all their fingers?" Tee demanded.

"I don't know. Hadn't thought about it."

"You stick your hand in the mouth of a snapping turtle that's about twice as big around as you are you're likely to draw back a bloody nub," Tee asserted.

"I guess some of them gents might not have had all their fingers, now that I think about it," Jim confessed.

◇

The next day Tee and Jim went about the business of gathering more-or-less round stones as close to the size of a mans head as they could find.

In the beginning they had no difficulty finding the desired size stones close enough to their building site to simply carry them in their hands and stack them into a crude fence.

Only a few feet of the fence had been completed when the nearby supply of stones was depleted.

The men then employed the tactic of gathering stones into small stacks and later returning with a team of mules hitched to a wagon, gathering the stones into the wagon and driving to the corral site and adding them to the fence.

After three weeks of working all the daylight hours the corral fence stood three feet tall forming a more-or-less circular enclosure having a diameter of about thirty feet.

"That ain't a very high fence," Jim observed.

"No it ain't," Tee replied. "I expect we'll have to hobble the stock to keep 'em in there, but that'll be a lot easier than building a high enough fence to keep "em in."

"I reckon tomorrow we can start on the feed shed," Jim observed.

"I reckon," Tee replied.

"What do you think to build it out of? There ain't enough timber in that river bottom in fifty miles to build an outhouse, let alone a feed shed," Jim said.

"Rocks," Tee replied. "We'll use then flat rocks about four inches thick, and stand 'em on edge to make a wall.

"When I was in the Mexican War down in Mexico I seen 'em making Adobe out of clay dirt, and I see there's an outcropping of clay in that river bank that I think will make a good enough Adobe to use to mortar them rocks into a fine wall."

"Ga-damned Tee, I sure as hell am tired of digging up rocks," Jim complained.

◇

The next morning the men began searching for four-inch thick stones that would fit together like pieces of a jigsaw puzzle.

It wasn't difficult to find four-inch thick stones, some lying on the surface, some partially buried; the difficult part was fitting them together in a wall.

At about mid morning on their third day of trying to fit together stones Jim said, pointing his nose off toward the southeast, "There's a man coming yonder."

Tee looked in the direction Jim was indicating and saw a man on horseback about a half a mile away heading in their direction.

"Think he's an Indian?" Tee asked.

"Judging from the hat he's wearing I'd say more likely a cowboy. I can't really tell from this distance," Jim replied.

"Why don't you wander on over to the tent and bring back our pistols, just in case," Tee suggested.

Tee stood watching the man ride in while he leaned on the handle of the shovel he'd been working with.

The man was about fifty yards out when Jim returned with the guns that each man stuffed into the waistband of his pants.

They could now see that the man was riding a long-legged

brown horse, and was wearing a wide-brimmed hat, a gray cotton work shirt with a red bandana tied loosely around his neck, denim britches, boots, and a very large pistol on his hip.

As the man came closer the men could see that the he was redheaded with broad shoulders with strong looking arms, and that he had large blue eyes set in a rectangular face who's skin was nearly as red as his hair.

At about ten yards the man reined his horse to a stop saying "Howdy," and surveying the scene asked, "What are you fellers building here?"

"We're building a stagecoach relay station for the Butterfield Overland Mail that's going to start up in about three months," Tee replied.

"I heard that Butterfield had made a deal with Mr. Nail to use a place up here somewhere.

"I cowboy for the Nail outfit. My name is Horace Jones. Everybody calls me Howdy."

"I'm Tee Wells, and this here is my brother Jim. Why don't you step down and stay awhile? We have some coffee over at the tent. We'd be glad for some company."

"Don't mind if I do," Howdy said, throwing his leg over the horse's rump and stepping lightly to the ground.

"From all them flat rocks you gents are digging up, I reckon you're building a house," Howdy observed, intending the remark as a question.

"Directly, but now we're building a feed shelter. Then we'll build a house and then a shelter for the stock," Tee replied.

◇

Reaching the tent the men made themselves comfortable setting on various wooden goods crates, sipping coffee from tin cups and making casual conversation.

When a silence fell between then Jim said, "Superintendent O'Donnell said this here country has two Indian reservations in it."

"Yeah, you have Caddos and Anadarkos to the east," Howdy said, swinging his hand holding his coffee cup to indicate the general direction, "and Wacos, Tawakonus, and Comanches," indicating the opposite direction with his coffee cup, "to the west."

"Comanches!" Tee exclaimed.

Howdy went on, "Yeah, it's hard to tell if the Indians are causing more trouble, or if the whites are causing more trouble."

"The whites claim that the Indians use the reservations to hide-out on and raid as they please, and the Indians claim it's white men doing the devilment and blaming it in them

"Either way, there's plenty of trouble brewing."

Howdy took a sip of his coffee, and continued, "Some of them settlers are about ready to march onto the reservations and kill every Indian in sight.

"And then there's talk that the Government is going to move the Indians to Indian Territory.

"I expect that by this time next year them Indians will be gone from this country, one way or the other," Howdy concluded.

"I don't hold with shooting down people who've dun no wrong, even if they are Indians," Tee offered. "But, I sure would rest a lot easier if the Indians were gone from here."

Draining his coffee cup, Jim assured, "We ain't had any trouble with 'em yet."

"I don't recon you gents are in any more danger here than you would be anywhere else out in this country," Howdy reasoned. "It ain't likely that the reservation Indians are the ones doing the meanness. It's the wild ones, and they're as likely to strike one place as another."

Howdy warned, "Them wild Indian will steal anything that ain't red-hot or nailed down, and will kill a white man in the meanest ways they can think of just because he's a white man, and they'll do worse than that to a white woman."

Howdy paused, taking another sip of coffee.

Jim rose from his seat and reaching for the coffee pot asked, "More coffee?"

Each man held his cup out for Jim to top-off.

Returning to his place, Jim addressed Howdy, "You know anything about an Army Post up the river?"

"Oh yeah, Old Camp Cooper[7]. You gents ought to go up there and get acquainted with the commander. He has a feller up there that knows how to bust out this limestone in regular shaped building blocks. If you could get him to show you how to do that it sure would be a lot easier that what you gents are trying to do," Howdy offered.

"Well, I sure am in favor of that," Jim asserted. "I'm beginning to wonder if I would have been better off to have robbed a bank and got myself sentenced to hard labor in the penitentiary than to have taken this job."

"Ah, come on Jim," Tee kidded. "It ain't all that bad."

And, addressing Howdy, "Thank you kindly for that suggestion Mr. Jones. We sure will take your advice on that."

◇

Tee and Jim were up long before sunup, having finished their coffee, bacon and biscuits. They loaded tools into the wagon to which they hitched two mules.

At first light they struck out, crossing the Clear Fork, climbing out of its valley onto the prairie, and turning upstream followed the rim of the river's valley according to Howdy's directions to find Old Camp Cooper.

By the time the Sun had climbed a hand above the eastern horizon the men stopped their wagon in front of the headquarters building.

Jim took his pipe from his pocket, and while tamping its bowl full of tobacco made a careful appraisal of the military post.

Old Camp Cooper, while supposedly a temporary encampment, was constructed in the style of many frontier military installations of its day having a large imposing headquarters building flanked on one side by a two-story home befitting the post commander, and on the other by a similarly styled unmarried officers quarters that was almost as large as the headquarters building. All of the buildings were constructed of limestone that glistened almost as white as snow in the early morning sun.

Jim drew a Lucifer from his pants pocket and struck it on his rump. Lit his pipe, shook the flame off the match, and started to toss it away, but thinking better of it made certain it was cold and put it into his pocket.

Across the parade ground stood a neat row of two-room houses facing the headquarters building. These were the housing for married officers. They too, were made of limestone.

A second tier of buildings in back of the married officers quarters was the barracks that housed the troops and noncommissioned officers.

Still further to the rear were stables, and standing off the ends of the parade ground were the hospital, quartermasters, bakery, guardhouse, armory, and other unidentifiable buildings.

All the buildings had been constructed with limestone walls, pitch roofs with shake shingles, and had the appearance of having come from the same cookie-cutter.

The living quarters were all equipped with a freestanding cookhouse that served to provide fire protection and to relieve the living quarters of some of the intense summer heat.

Having finished his appraisal, Jim pointed the stem of his pipe to the headquarters building and commented, "I recon the man we need to see is in there."

Tee tied the lines (reins) to the break handle and climbed down from the wagon.

Entering the headquarters building the men found a lieutenant manning a desk who called, "Can I help you gents?"

Tee replied, "We wanted to make the acquaintance of the post commander."

"He's out on patrol. You'll have to come back another time," the lieutenant stated.

"There's another thing, maybe you can help us out with. We were told you have a man up here that knows how to quarry this limestone so it comes out in blocks suitable to building," Tee said.

Letting a touch of impatience creep into his question the lieutenant asked, "And?"

Tee replied, "We're building a stagecoach relay station for the Butterfield Overland Mail down the river about eight miles, and being as there ain't no wood in this country we thought we would build out of stone. So, it'd be a big help if your man could show us how to quarry that limestone."

"We've received orders to cooperate with Butterfield," the lieutenant said, with a sharp tone to his voice. "There's a work detail making up out in the Parade Ground now that's going to quarry stone. Go out there and find Sergeant Moorhead, and tell him I said for him to show you gents how they cut the stone."

"Thank you lieutenant," Tee said. "Please tell the commander we came by, and if you fellers are down our way stop in for a visit."

"Good morning gentlemen," the lieutenant said dismissively.

◇

Sergeant Moorhead, while strictly military, proved to be an accommodating man.

"You can't do too much at a time," he said, showing the men how to use a star bit and sledge to drill holes in the stone, and a cold chisel to scribe the surface where he intended the fracture to occur.

When five holes had been drilled at strategic locations Moorhead poured gunpowder into them, then rigged a fuse, and tamped sand on top of the gunpowder.

"Always use a wooden dowel to tamp powder with," Moorhead advised. "A steel rod would work easier, but it might strike a spark and blow that powder up right in your face."

"Now, if you can get all the shots to go off at the same time you'll get a real good result," Moorhead assured.

The shots were fired and the stone fractured more or less along the lines Moorhead had scribed into them yielding four usable blocks of limestone.

"I never can get all them damned shots to go off just right," Moorhead grumped.

By the end of the day Tee and Jim were on their way back to Clear Fork Station confident that they could quarry the stone they needed to build the structures they required.

◇

The next morning Tee located an outcropping of limestone he deemed suitable a couple of hundred yards from their building site.

He prepared a request for roofing material to be forwarded to Mr. O'Donnell by the next company man to come by, and he and Jim got to work quarrying stone.

The stone came out of the ground in rectangular blocks generally about six times the size of an ordinary brick.

The process was slow and tedious, but Tee was pleased with the outcome and was certain the stone would work into a strong wall when they were employed in the fashion that bricks are made into structures.

The walls were finished two days before the roofing material arrived thus giving the men only a brief respite before it was back to construction work for both of them.

The feed shed was finished in late August.

At its completion Jim suggested, "We ought to move our quarters into the shed. It would be a lot better than that tent."

Tee agreed, "Yeah. I think you're right."

The men took some time to hunt and fish, but with all the Indians forging in the area there was little game to be found, so after five days they started quarrying stone for their house.

◇

With the feed shed and corral finished, Mike O'Donnell appeared as if on cue with wagons loaded with feed, hay, harness, a month worth of supplies, and six extra mules.

Bringing the caravan to a stop and inspecting the handiwork of Tee and Jim, O'Donnell asserted, "I'll declare, if that ain't the best looking damned feed shed in the whole Texas Division. Where in the world did you gents get them snow-white stones?"

"We quarried it yonder," Tee announced, pointing in the direction of their quarry.

"You gents will have a fine looking station here if you make your house and other buildings out of that stone," O'Donnell asserted.

"With you dropping off feed and mules, I suppose we're about to get started in the stagecoach and mail business" Tee observed.

"Yes, we expect to start the first mail from St. Louis on September 16th. The schedule calls for the first coach to pass here on the 23rd," O'Donnell stated.

◇

In mid afternoon on September 22, 1858 Tee noticed a cloud of dust rising off the plain about a mile north of the station.

Watching for a few seconds, he saw a wagon with a canvas top[8] being pulled by six mules running at a slow gallop come into focus.

"Lookie yonder," Tee said to Jim, pointing to the wagon.

Jim taking a long look, asked, "Is that the mail coming?"

"Yeah I expect we'd better get them mules hitched. They'll be here in a few minutes," Tee replied.

"They're a full day ahead of schedule," Jim marveled.

"Let's get going. We don't want to hold 'em up any."

◇

When the driver stopped the wagon the only passenger stepped down and introduced himself as Waterman L. Ormsby,[9*] Special Correspondent for the New York Herald.

Mr. Ormsby chatted with Tee and Jim while the teams were being exchanged revealing that he intended to accompany the first mail all the way from St. Louis to San Francisco, and to write reports of the trip for the New York Herald to be published in a series of articles.

He also commented on the difficulty he was having sleeping on the bench seats who's backs could be lowered into a flat surface on which the passenger was expected to roll himself in blankets to sleep.

When the fresh team was hitched the driver and Ormsby resumed their respective seats, and the driver cracked the whip over the mules heads causing them to bolt into a gallop, with their hooves kicking gravel and dust into the faces of Tee and Jim as the wagon clamored away.

The driver called over his shoulder, "See you boys in about a week."

Tee and Jim stood watching the wagon disappear into the distance, both having a look of dismay on their faces.

"I expected to see one of them Concord Coaches, like the ones they use back east," Jim said absently.

"I guess the wagons will be easier to pull and more stable on these rough trails in this country," Tee speculated.

"They sure weren't here long," Jim observed.

"No. And only one passenger. It sure don't look like we're going to be selling much of anything to the passengers," Tee replied.

After a moments thought, Tee said, "I reckon we might as well get on out to the quarry and get us a load of limestone so we can get to work on our house."

"I reckon," Jim replied unenthusiastically.

◇

While driving the wagon to the quarry Tee mused, "I wonder if it would be a good idea to put in a general store out here?

"I expect there's probably eight or ten settlers within seven or eight miles of the station and there will be more coming in as time goes on, and it sure don't look like we'll be selling much to the passengers with only two mail wagons a week, and if we have a general store we can still sell to whatever passengers there is."

"That'll take a bigger building than just a house," Jim asserted.

"Yeah, it will," Tee agreed. "I suppose if we don't spend any of our pay till we get it built we'll have enough to buy stock to get started."

"I reckon we won't have no trouble saving our money. There sure ain't no place out here to spend it," Jim observed.

Jim drew his pipe from his pocket, tamped the bowl full of tobacco, and lit up.

After a couple of thoughtful draws on the pipe he said, "There's one other thing."

"What's that?" Tee asked.

"Its gotta have a side room with some card tables and a bar."

Tee gave Jim a sideways look, and with a knowing smile, said, "That'll take an even bigger building."

◇

After a few weeks the men fell into a routine of going to quarry early in the day, working there until noon, returning to the station, unloading the wagon, digging clay for mortar, and fitting the stones into the walls of their building.

They made it a practice to bring more material than they would use in one day in order to allow them to work a full day at the station on the days the mail wagons were due to pass.

◇

By mid December the men had the building exterior and roof complete and were able to concentrate their labor on finishing the interior and acquiring stock.

Their first order to a supplier was for whisky. "Men don't need no gingham and lace," Jim argued.

◇

On the second Monday in February 1859 Tee and Jim declared The Clear Fork Station General Store and Saloon open for business.

The building was twenty-five feet by twenty feet. The front was made to face east, and sported a covered gallery with benches and chairs on it.

The north and south ends of the building were gabled and there was a fireplace in each. There were two windows in each end, and four windows and two doors on the east side of the building.

The roof was equipped with two cupolas that could be opened in summer to allow heat to escape, and closed in winter to hold heat in.

The store occupied a twelve-foot by twelve-foot room in the northeast corner of the building, and the saloon occupied an equal space in the southeast corner. The back was divided into two rooms each eight feet by twelve feet. One room being their kitchen and sleeping quarters and the other being storage.

The store was equipped with shelves around its perimeter. There was a counter parallel to the back wall with jars of stick candy on one end and a roll of brown wrapping paper on a frame that included a paper cutter and a spool of twine string for wrapping and tying packages of goods

There were catalogues spread on the counter from which customers could order items that weren't carried by the store with a sign over them stating, "All Orders Are Guaranteed To Arrive Within Six Months."

The bar in the saloon sat facing the front door with shelves containing bottles and glasses behind it.

The bar was made of sawed planks nailed to the bottom of two overturned wooden barrels. In the beginning it didn't have a foot-rail, but one was added in the next year.

Three card-tables were in the front of the room, each having four chairs and a brass spittoon. There were three more spittoons at the bar.

There was no mirror behind the bar, nor were there any paintings or decorations anywhere in the room save for a calendar that a whisky drummer left.

The first two days were a complete bust. No one came.

A little past noon on Wednesday Howdy Jones rode his long legged horse up to the hitching post out front, dismounted, tied up, and came stomping into the saloon speaking in his outdoor voice, "Howdy gents. I sure as hell am glad to see you fellers put this saloon in here, wy' it's the only watering hole 'tween here and Belknap. Gimme a whisky, Tee."

"We're real glad to see you Howdy. This is the third day we've been open and you're the first customer we've seen, so the first drink is on us," Tee said.

"Hallelujah, I'm always glad to have a free drink," Howdy asserted as he savored the glass of amber liquid.

"Not only are you our first customer, that tip you gave us about Old Camp Cooper and learning to quarry that limestone has been a real help to us," Jim praised.

"Yes, it was," Tee, agreed. "Have another drink on us on account of your giving us that tip."

"Hallelujah again," Howdy crowed.

Taking time to look the saloon over, Howdy then offered, "You gents need to build a bigger place than this, wy' there's more than enough cowboys working on the Nail to fill this place up, and you'll have 'em coming in here from twenty miles around."

Having finished the second drink Howdy said, "Now let me buy you fellers a drink, and we'll drink to your success. I sure am glad to see this here saloon in here."

◇

Howdy was overly optimistic about the number of patrons the store and saloon would draw.

On Saturday nights a few cowboys would show up to play poker and drink, but the profits were so meager that Tee and Jim wouldn't have bothered to stay open if it were not for the fact that they had sunk their last dollar into the inventory.

On one Saturday night a couple of the cowboys from different ranches got into such a heated argument over the card game that Tee fetched his sawed-off double-barreled 12 gage in readiness to put a stop to it if he had to, but cooler heads prevailed in the end.

The incident was tense enough to provoke Tee and Jim to agree not to allow armed men in the saloon and to that end they put a sign over the bar that stated, "If You Want To Drink Handover Your Pistols to The Bartender."

At first some of the cowboys were put off by the rule, but they soon decided that if no one was armed then no one needed to be armed, and that they would rather drink than argue.

◇

The store hadn't been setup as a trading post and held little interest to the Indians except for the whisky, which was illegal for them to buy.

The goods furnished to the Indians by the Indian Agents were meeting their needs.

Even though it was illegal to sell whisky to Indians, and illegal for them to buy it, that didn't keep the Indians from trying to acquire spirits by whatever means they could.

Tee was suspicious that some of the cowboys were buying whisky and trading it to the Indians for various goods, and in some cases the use of their squaws as prostitutes.

On an afternoon in mid April when the east-bound mail was due Tee started to the corral to hitch the mules when he saw Charlie Paddlefoot, a Comanche from the reservation, slink away from beside the feed shed with a jug of whisky in his hand.

Nearing the feed shed he heard the sounds of a man and woman coupling emitting from inside.

"Come out of there, the both of you," Tee ordered.

In a few moments a cowboy that Tee knew only as Harry and Charlie Paddlefoot's squaw emerged.

Harry was angry. The squaw was completely blank-faced.

"Damn you Wells," Harry snarled. "I traded a full jug for this squaw, and you come along and bust-in in the middle of things and wreck the whole deal."

"You know it's against the law to sell or trade whisky to Indians, and even if it wasn't you ought to be ashamed to dally with their women," Tee asserted.

"Damn you Wells, I'll dally as I please, and you do the same."

"You do your dallying, and your whisky drinking somewhere besides here. Now, get from here, and don't come back."

Turning to the woman Tee commanded, "And you, squaw, tell Charlie Paddlefoot not to come back here either."

◇

On the last Saturday in May, Howdy and three other cowboys were playing poker and talking about the recent goings on it the Clear Fork Country.

"You gents hear about that bunch out of Jack County coming over here to mob the Indians?" Cleve asked the party of players while the cards were being dealt.

"Yeah, I heard they was under the leadership of that Baylor[10] fellow that use to be the Indian Agent back in fifty-five (1855)," Bill allowed.

"The Army got wind of what Baylor was up to and put a stop to it before they got onto the reservation." Cleve offered while studying his cards.

"I'd kinda hate to see something like that happen," Howdy said, eyeing his cards with a blank expression. "But, I sure would be glad to see them Indians gone from this country."

"I expect everybody around here would be glad to see them Indians gone," the fourth man said, and pitched a dime on the table saying, "It'll cost you boys a dime to play poker with me."

Calling the bet, "Damn, them cards must like you tonight," Howdy grouched as he pitched his dime on the table.

"I don't expect that'll be the end of it," Bill observed, pitching his cards face down on the table. "Baylor ain't gonna quit 'till he gets his way about things."

"He sure don't make no secret of how much he hates Indians," Cleve observed, and added his dime to the pot.

"Yeah, he hates Indians nearly as much as he hates that Indian Agent, Major Neighbors[11]," Bill added before taking a drink from his glass of whisky.

"Baylor's got plenty of company when it comes to hatein' Neighbors," Cleve asserted taking a drink before going on. "All them trading post operators up on the Red River, and every land speculator in the country, and most of the settlers, all despise Neighbors for the way he coddles his pet Indians on the reservation."

"Well, I sure hope it can all get settled before anything else happens," Howdy commented. "The way I hear it, Baylor came close to starting a war with the Army. We sure don't need anything like that starting around here."

The dealer lay his hand of cards face down on the table, picked up the deck, and asked, "How many cards do you gents want?"

◇

On a Saturday late afternoon in the middle of June, a day when the temperature had gone over a-hundred degrees in the shade, Howdy was the first customer to appear at the Clear Fork Station Saloon.

If Tee hadn't seen him a dozen times before it would have been difficult to imagine Howdy's bowlegged stomping amble as he came into the saloon calling, "Gimme a whisky Tee. I swear it's hotter than the hubs of hell out there today."

"Glad to see you Howdy," Tee said while pouring a glass of whisky, and setting it on the bar.

Howdy took a good swallow of the amber liquid, and wiped his mouth on his sleeve with a sigh of approval.

"Whatta ye been up to lately? Tee asked, absently wiping the bar with a towel.

"Ah, just trying to keep them jug-headed cows more or less on the home range, same as usual."

Howdy took another drink, and continued, "Just come from up towards the Comanche camp. Big doings going on up there."

"They getting' ready to bust out?" Tee asked anxiously.

"No, no! The Army is getting' ready to move 'em to Indian Territory."

"But them Indians are hoppin' mad though. The Army is making them move off from good crops in their fields and they're making 'em leave their livestock and all their belongings 'sept what they can carry on their backs."

"I'm real glad to have them Indians gone from this country, but it ain't' right to do 'em that way," Tee argued. "Some of them Indians have worked real hard learning to farm and ranch, and have tried to learn white man ways."

Howdy finished his drink and held up the empty glass to indicate he wanted it filled, saying as he did so, "Na it ain't right to do 'em that way, but I guess that's the wisdom of our Government at work."

CHAPTER 3

A Handful of Stars

The eastbound mail wagon was due around noon and now with it nearing sundown the wagon was still nowhere in sight.

A dark wall of clouds were in sight off to the northwest, and were rumbling with thunder and moving in on the station.

The rain started with a blast. The storm was punctuated with sharp gusts of wind, claps of thunder, and pea-size hail.

It rained torrents for a full three minutes, and then as quickly as it had started it was gone leaving in its wake a vivid rainbow stretching from horizon to horizon that lasted only a few minutes before the sun set.

The storm-front left behind clean, cold, air that lay on the land as still as death.

"That didn't amount to much," Jim observed.

"No, it didn't," Tee replied. "Lets have supper and then I'll go out and watch for the eastbound."

"All right, I have a report for O'Donnell I need to get finished before the eastbound gets here, if I can," Jim announced.

While Tee made a pot of coffee Jim brought a canvas bag filled with jerked venison in it and a jar of honey from the cupboard. Tee dipped a couple of bowls of beans from a pot near the fire.

There were always beans. Even for breakfast, there were beans.

The men dredged the jerked venison in the honey and ate it with their fingers. They ate the beans with a spoon, and washed it all down with coffee that they drank from tin cups

The meal finished, Jim poured himself another cup of coffee and leaning back in his chair started loading his pipe.

"I think I'll go on out and watch for the eastbound. I should be able to spot its running lights when it tops that rise this side of Stony Creek and that'll give me plenty of time to harness the team before they get here," Tee commented.

"I'll be out directly," Jim replied.

◇

Tee had been standing with his arms resting on the corral gate long enough that full darkness had arrived. The night was crisp, clear, and still in the wake of the thunderstorm and with no moon the stars were visible to the horizon in all directions. Some of the stars were so bright they cast shadows.

Tee looked up into the heavens observing that the stars looked close enough that he could touch them.

Now wouldn't it be a sight if I picked a handful of those stars and sprinkled them in Lela's hair. Yes'er that would surly be a sight.

"Oh Lela! Will you ever stop haunting me?"

Tee didn't realize that he had spoken aloud until he heard Jim say from in back of him, "Tee you shouldn't let your mind run on that. You know how melancholy it makes you every time you think about all them doings."

"She just comes unbidden, out of nowhere. I expect I'll never get rid of the memories of her.

"Sometimes I think I'd make a deal with the Devil to have her," Tee remarked.

"They's already been one St. Theophilus[12]. I don't expect you'll be the second," Jim said wryly.

Tee chuckled a mirthless chuckle, "No brother Jim, if you don't put me up for sainthood I don't expect anybody else will.

"I might as well make a deal with Satan though, I've already put myself in hell when I promised Lela I'd walk away if she chose Charlie over me, which was mighty damned stupid of me. But unlike St. Theophilus who got what he wanted and then reneged on old Satan, I can't renege on Lela, or I won't renege on her."

"You walked away. It's a long way from here to Cairo, Illinois," Jim observed.

"I walked away in body only," Tee replied regretfully. "Only in body, brother Jim."

"Put all that out of your mind and pay attention to that mail wagon coming yonder and let's get them mules harnessed," Jim said.

Tee said, speaking as much to himself as to Jim, "I think I'll ride that wagon on over to Belknap and spend a few days. Every thing is running good around here so you wont miss me for a few days."

"You might as well, you won't be worth a damned around here with Lela on your mind.

"There's some mighty rough old chippies around Belknap with Fort Belknap there and all, so you watch your doings and come on back here directly," Jim admonished.

"I'll be back, and then you can take a few days over there if you please," Tee replied.

◇

In nine days Tee returned on the westbound mail wagon.

He stepped down from the wagon, exchanged greetings with Jim, and went to work helping exchange the teams of mules in order to expedite the departure of the mail.

"Have a good time in town?" Jim asked when the wagon was on its way.

"I was having a pretty good time until I saw a man gunned down in an alley. Shot in the back with a shotgun, the gent that used to be the Indian Agent named Major Robert Neighbors[13].

Changing the subject, Tee asked, "Do you have any coffee brewed up? I'm as dry as powder after that wagon ride."

"There's coffee, and beans too, if you want 'em,' Jim replied, and then asked, That feller that you saw shot a Major in the Army, was'e?"

"He was a Major in the Army of The Republic of Texas awhile back. Then he was the Indian Agent on the reservations that were over here on the Clear Fork till they moved the Indians to Indian Territory."

Tee continued as the men walked toward their house, saying, "The talk around the saloons in Belknap was that that gent named Baylor got crossways with Neighbors back in fifty-five (1855) when he blamed Neighbors for his getting fired as Indian Agent, and Neighbors taking his place. They've been bickering ever since with Baylor saying the Indians were stealing cattle and horses, and Neighbors saying it was Baylor and his henchmen that were doing the stealing, and blaming it on the Indians."

When the men were in the house Jim poured two cups of coffee and setting one before Tee asked, "Baylor do the shooting, did'e?"

"No, He was in the courthouse with the sheriff and a judge when the shooting took place, but all the talk around the saloons have it that it was one of his men that did it," said Tee.

Taking a sip of coffee, he then went on, "Baylor's the one that led that mob out of Jack county that started over here in May to wipe out the Indians, and they say Neighbors is the one that put the Army on him for that stunt."

"You see the man that done the shooting?" Jim asked.

"All I saw was his back. I was walking down the sidewalk, and just as I stepped across the alley I heard the shotgun blast a few feet away and saw Neighbors fall and the man with the gun run on out the other end of the alley. He was a stocky man about my height is all I could tell the sheriff, but the sheriff said I'd better keep a sharp eye out, that the bunch that run with Baylor are mighty rough and are likely to come make sure I can't tell any more than I have," Tee concluded.

Each man took a sip of coffee and Jim asked, "Will you know him if he comes?"

"No, all I ever saw of him was his back. I told the sheriff I wouldn't know if he was standing in front of me."

"What do you think to do?" Jim asked.

"Keep a sharp eye out, and go armed, all the time," Tee answered.

Both men stared idly at the corners of the room sipping their coffee, when after a few moments of contemplation Jim replied, "I reckon that's about all there is to be done alright."

◇

On Saturday evening several of the cowboys from nearby ranches were drinking and playing a friendly game of five-card when Howdy Jones came in shouting, "Howdy boys, I'm here now, the partying can start.

"Tee, gim'e a whisky.

"I hear you been over to Belknap a few days back. Did you see my girlfriend over there?"

"I don't know Howdy. What's your girlfriend's name?" Tee asked as he poured a drink and set it before Howdy.

"Roseanne. She works in the Trailhead Saloon."

"I don't reckon I did. I don't think I ever got that far down the trail. Anyway, I don't remember it if I did," Tee confessed.

"I know it's a damned fool thing," Howdy said, looking down at the drink before him. "I'd marry that girl if she'd have me, but she said I couldn't afford to keep her the way she's got used to."

Looking up at Tee, Howdy continued, "Wy' you know she told me she makes more than twenty dollars a day working in that saloon, and I make thirty dollars a month cowboyin'."

Howdy downed his drink and gestured for Tee to pour another, and went on saying, "I tell you Tee, it's a damned shame I wasn't born a woman. There sure enough would've been a whore in my daddy's family if I had been. It sure would beat the hell out of this damned cowboyin'."

After another whisky Howdy moved over to the card game and continued buying drinks and hooraying all the other players about who had the fastest horse and who could ride the roughest bronc.

"Awhile back I's over on Lambs Head Creek looking for strays," Howdy was saying to the men gathered around the card game, "and I seen a sheep over there that looked just like ol' Cleve there."

A round of chuckles followed.

"A fellow over in Jacksboro told me the only place they get virgin wool is from sheep that can outrun the shepherd," another card player chimed in provoking another round of laughter.

"You know, I figure if them cows could outrun ol' Jones here, there wouldn't be so damned many red cows around here," Cleve shot back.

Another round of laughter.

"Oh, Cleve I don't have to resort to such things as that, I've got me a fine woman over by Fort Belknap," Howdy asserted.

"You mean that little chippie I seen you patting on the butt in the Trailhead Saloon the last time I was over there?" Cleve asked.

The mood around the table suddenly went somber as Howdy answered tersely, "Yow, that's the one I mean."

The tension was eased somewhat when George Baker, one of the card players, said calmly, "The bet's a half-dime to you Howdy."

Staring daggers through Cleve, "Call," Howdy said sharply.

◇

Howdy lost more hands than he won, but he was having a good time and getting drunker by the hour.

Close to midnight when the game broke up Howdy announced that he was going to Belknap to see Roseanne for the rest of the weekend.

Tee wondered how he had enough money left to make the trip worthwhile.

"None of my business, he'll probably sober up on the way and turn and go on home," Tee thought.

CHAPTER 4

Bad Men, Bad Indians, and Four good Women

On the next Tuesday morning Tee and Jim were up and had finished the breakfast of beans, biscuits, and coffee before sunup.

"I'll take a water barrel on the sled and go down to the river and bring back water for the stock," Jim volunteered.

"While you're doing that I'll cleanup in here and then I'll go out and start feeding the stock," Tee replied.

When Jim returned he stopped the mules that were pulling the sled near the feed shed, not adjacent to the water trough where the water he had hauled up from the river was needed.

Stepping off the sled Jim held a finger over his lips signaling Tee to remain silent, and with his other hand he beckoned for Tee to come to him.

What the hell is this all about? Tee puzzled as he walked toward Jim.

When Tee came near, Jim said, "There's a man laying out yonder by that dry wash watching us.

"You can't see him from here because the shed is between him and us, but he's laying beside that little mesquite bush where the dry wash makes a turn toward the river."

"What do you reckon he's up to?" Tee asked.

"All I could see is he's just laying there watching. I didn't see a horse anywhere he might have rode in on," Jim replied.

"Lets wander over to the house, and when we get there I'll take the shotgun and go out the other side and down to the river and then I can work my way up that draw to within a few feet of him before he knows I'm there," Tee appraised.

"You can get yourself shot doing a stunt like that," Jim argued.

"If he's got a rifle he can shoot both of us from where he is if that's what he wants to do," Tee returned.

"Maybe we're too jumpy. Maybe somebody needs help, but I don't hanker to go walking straight up to him without knowing what he's up to," Tee reasoned.

"I guess he could be an Indian come to steal horses since I can't see a horse he rode in on," Jim mused.

"You can cover 'em with the rifle from inside the house while I work my way around to 'em. He won't be able to see you when you're inside in the shadows," Tee observed.

◇

It took most of an hour for Tee to work his way down the river bottom to the dry wash, and then up the wash, making as little noise as possible, finally coming to within a few feet of the man lying in the dry wash.

Reasoning that he could get no closer without giving himself away, Tee sprang up bringing his double-barreled twelve-gauge to bear on the man and calling in command tone, "Don't move mister."

Mister did not obey.

Mister rolled onto his back bringing his rifle to bear on Tee. Both guns fired simultaneously.

Tee's 00 buckshot loads shredded Mister's upper abdomen and lower chest. Fountains of blood erupted from some of the wounds while streams of blood flowed from others.

Mister's rifle shot caught Tee in his left side knocking him down and breaking two ribs on its way through his side, luckily missing the lung.

Jim broke from the house running as fast as he could, shouting as he came, "Tee are you hurt?"

Tee drew his pistol from his belt against the possibility that Mister would rise and try to shoot him again.

"Who are you, and what do you want here?" Tee called to Mister.

Mister made an unintelligible reply and perished.

"Tee, are you hurt?" Jim called as he came running with the rifle at the ready.

"I'm hit in the side, but I don't think it's mortal, but it sure hurts like hell" Tee replied when Jim was close enough that he didn't have to strain to answer.

"What happened?" Jim asked.

"When I ordered him not to move he swung his rifle on me and I had to shoot 'em," Tee replied painfully.

"He's dead, ain't he?" Jim questioned.

"Yes."

"You know him?"

"No."

"You think he's the one that shot Neighbors?"

"Could be I reckon. He's about the same size and dressed a lot like that gent was," Tee replied.

Jim examined Tee's wound and observed, "You're not bleeding much. Do you think you can walk? Or, do you want me to bring the sled over here so you can ride back to the house?"

"I can walk if you let me lean on you some, but you'll need the sled to get him over where you're going to bury him. I don't think I'm up to digging right now," Tee advised.

After a moments thought, Tee said, "Why don't you go through his pockets? Maybe you'll find something to identify him."

Jim found a pocketknife, a pocket watch with a picture of a woman in it, twelve dollars in money, and a wanted poster bearing Mister's picture.

The wanted poster gave his name as Thaddeus Simpson, wanted in Erath County on suspicion of cattle rustling. There was no reward offered.

◇

Jim helped Tee to the house and into bed.

"Do you think I ought to hitch the mules to the wagon and take you to the doctor?" Jim asked.

"Not now. I don't know how bad I'm wounded, but it hurts too much to think about riding a wagon for thirty miles.

"You go on and get Mister buried, and then we'll decide if I ought to go to the doctor." Tee said.

◇

By the time Jim returned from burying Mister, Tee had decided that he had two broken ribs and that Jim could bandage them as well as a doctor could.

"Next time we're over to Jacksboro I'll let the doc take a look at me if I ain't healed proper by then," Tee concluded.

Jim went about the task of writing a letter to the sheriff detailing all the particulars of the killing of Mister.

He bundled Mister's belongings along with the letter and sent the package to the sheriff on the next eastbound mail wagon.

◇

Four weeks later the sheriff stopped by to ask numerous questions about the shooting of Simpson

Tee and Jim told him everything they knew about the incident including their speculation as to whether he was the man who shot Major Neighbors and the fact that they hadn't found the horse he was riding.

"Well, the horse probably wandered off, we may find it, or we may not. I expect he was the one that shot Neighbors, alright," the sheriff commented. "He was on my list of likely culprits, and he run with that Baylor bunch, so I expect he done the shooting alright, but you're not out of the woods on this yet Tee, he has a brother who'll be coming to see all about what happened.

"One good thing is that the family lives way off over in East Texas somewhere, so it may take several months before the brother hears about Thad being dead."

The sheriff visited on for another hour with the conversation turned to more casual topics before he got to his feet saying, "Well gents, I guess I'd better get saddled up and head on back home, it'll be dark before I get there now."

"Stay the night if you please," Jim offered.

"Oh no, I need to get on back to town, maybe another time."

Tee and Jim followed the sheriff to the porch of the store where they watched him mount his horse, and when he was mounted he asked, "Say, do you fellers know a cowboy around here named Howdy Jones?"

"Yeah, he's one of our best customers. He was a big help telling us about Old Camp Cooper when we first came here to build the station, heck of a good old boy."

"Is he now?" the sheriff mused.

"Oh yeah, we think a lot of Howdy. Why are you asking about him? He didn't give you no trouble over in town did'e?" Tee asked.

"No, no trouble, he's been spending a lot of time with a mighty expensive gal over at the Trailhead, probably nothing to concern the law. It's just that he's been spending too much money for a working cowboy, just wondering where he was getting it, is all," the sheriff replied.

"He plays cards here some. Wins some. That must be where he's getting any more than his wages," Jim volunteered.

"That's probably it, probably where he's getting it alright.

"You gents taker easy, I'll see you another time," the sheriff called as he turned his horse and headed toward the river crossing.

◇

On a pleasant evening in the spring of 1860 at their new home near Fort Sill, Indian Territory Charlie Paddlefoot addressed a gathering of his friends. Men who in the past had been his comrades in arms, men who were now his comrades in misery listened as he spoke.

"Tonight I will ride to the Clear Fork country to kill white men. They have lied to me and cheated me for the last time."

The men sat cross-legged around a small fire near the lodge of Charlie Paddlefoot.

"They lied to us all when they told us we could be farmers in the Clear Fork Reservations and then when we had good crops in the ground, and herds of horses and cattle, they forced us to leave it all behind to come here to this desert where they said they would feed us and care for us, and instead they kill our friend Neighbors so he can help us no more and they leave us here to starve and to die like flies.

"We mean no more to them than flies. But, they will remember me, and they will be sorry they lied to me."

Charlie was taller than his fellow braves with hawk-like features, long sinewy arms and legs that bespoke athletic agility. Even seated, he could see over the heads of the others seated with him.

He spoke with fury in his voice, "I go to kill as many as I can. I will kill white men until they kill me. I will not come back to this place to live worse off than the white man's dog."

He paused, giving the others an opportunity to respond, but no one did.

"Any who come with me you can come back when you please, but I will not come back."

He paused again, waiting for response. But, none came.

"When the moon is down tonight come to my lodge. We will go when the solders can't see us ride away."

◇

Four others rode with Charlie.

Hawks, so called because his father was a white man named Hawkins, was an angry young man of twenty-two summers who fancied himself an accomplished knife fighter. No one considered it wise to argue the point with him.

Bat Ears, not the brightest star in the sky, but a loyal and obedient follower.

Eagle Claw, a man in his mid twenties whose left hand had been severely burned in childhood leaving it frozen in a claw-like posture.

Eagle Claw was the only member of the party who was armed with a firearm, an ancient musket for which he had enough powder and ball for five shots.

Wolf Scat, a boy of fourteen summers who received his name in his fifth summer when a wolf approached the village he shooed it away by shouting, "scat." A word he had learned from white traders.

The adults of the village thought the incident was hilarious, and thereafter he was Wolf Scat.

Over Charlie's objections to his going on the raid because of his youth and inexperience Wolf Scat argued, "I have not killed white men, nor have I known the pleasure of their women. If I don't go now I may never get another chance."

Charlie reasoned, "We go on this raid to die. Do you wish to die so young?"

"If I die on this raid, I will die as a brave, not as a fly."

◇

An hour after sunup on their third day out the raiding party sat on their ponies atop a low hill overlooking the Clear Fork country that had been part of the Comanche Reservation.

Three hundred yards distant they could see a settler's homestead that consisted of a picket house, and a cow-pen with a lean-to shelter for the livestock.

They could see three woman and four children near the cow-pen. The women were busy unhitching horses from a buggy and putting them into the pen.

"I don't see any men down there," Bat Ears observed.

"There are horses, and there will be food, and guns, and perhaps some whisky," Charlie announced.

"And there are three woman," Eagle Claw said, smiling at Wolf Scat.

◇

At the moment the Indians put their ponies into motion the woman took notice of them approaching.

They hurriedly gathered their children and ran to the house bolting the door behind them.

The Indians walked their ponies toward the house watching carefully for armed men to appear, or for guns to appear from windows or peep-holes in the house.

◇

The inmates in the house were; Mrs. Ward Phillips, the settler's wife, and her six-year-old son. Mrs. Phillips was a large breasted, dumpy, middle-aged woman.

Rebecca Miller the nineteen-year-old sister-in-law of the third woman and the mother of a six-month-old girl. Rebecca had long auburn hair and was strikingly beautiful.

Marian Miller was the mother of a seven-year-old boy and a five-year-old girl and she too was an attractive woman in her mid twenties.

Knowing that Mr. Phillips was away on business the Miller women, who now found themselves locked in terror, had driven to Mrs. Phillip's home to visit for the day.

◇

The five braves sat on their ponies in front of the house for several minutes without making any sound or attempting to entice the women to open the door or to come out.

Finally Charlie Paddlefoot dismounted and went to the door and knocked, calling, "Open door. We know you in there."

"No. I have a gun. You go away," Mrs. Phillips asserted.

"Want food. Want whisky. Open door."

"You go away from the door and I'll set food out, but no whisky," Mrs. Phillips replied.

Charlie Paddlefoot returned to his horse and in the Comanche language told Wolf Scat, "You find an iron tool and rip some boards off the house and go in and unbar the door for us."

Having found a suitable tool Wolf Scat pried two pickets off the house and crawled through the opening to be met by Mrs. Phillips holding a pistol on him.

Seeing that she was about to shoot the boy, Rebecca Miller grabbed the gun out of her hand, saying, "They only want food. There's no need for us to resist with force."

Mrs. Phillips then picked up a sadiron and swung it viciously with the intent of striking Wolf Scat on the head.

He saw the blow coming in time to dodge away enough that she hit him a glancing blow on his left shoulder.

Before she had time for another swing, Wolf Scat struck her savagely in the face knocking her down. She fell upon a bed that was nearby where she lay stunned by the blow.

The two Miller woman and their children huddled on the far side of the room while Wolf Scat opened the door for the other braves to enter.

"She hit me with an iron," Wolf Scat announced when the others were in the house.

Charlie Paddlefoot looked sternly at Wolf Scat and said, "Kill 'er."

Seeing Wolf Scat's surprise at the order he continued, "We came to kill whites, so start with her. She's too old to be of any pleasure and seeing her killed will take the fight out of the other two."

Mrs. Phillips, having recovered enough to assume a sitting position on the bed watched as Wolf Scat drew an arrow from his quiver, aimed at her, and loosed the arrow.

The arrow struck her in her right breast, skated around the breastbone, its head exiting under her right arm while the shaft remained in her body.

She cried out, but didn't try to move, nor did she faint.

"She's not dead," Eagle Claw cried. "Shoot her again!"

Wolf Scat drew another arrow from his quiver and shot the poor woman a second time.

The arrow entered her right breast about an inch from the first, and it too was deflected by her breastbone and exited under her right arm near the first.

Upon receiving the second arrow Mrs. Phillips fell on her left side lying on the bed where she had been seated.

Pretending to be dead, she lay motionless with her eyes open only the narrowest slit and offered a silent prayer that the savages would molest her no more.

"You killed her. Are you not going to scalp her?" Hawks chided. "You can borrow my knife, if you need one."

"I have a knife." Wolf Scat replied.

Realizing that she was going to be scalped, Mrs. Phillips determined to maintain her pretext of death, and steeling herself against the pain, she succeeded in the ruse.

At the last moment of the ordeal, when Wolf Scat ripped her scalp from her skull, Mrs. Phillips felt a wave of darkness sweeping over her. She prayed that God would forgive her tormenters, as she had, and fully expecting to awaken standing before Heavens Gates, she embraced the swoon.

During the entire atrocity the Miller woman had stood cowed hiding the children's faces in their skirts so that they wouldn't witness the barbarity.

Having finished with Mrs. Phillips, the Indians turned to ransacking the house in search of food, guns, and whisky; all of which they found.

When they finished their plunder, the Indians herded the Miller women and the children to horses where they tied all of them onto the horse's backs.

With their prisoners secured, the party struck a trail into the wilderness south of Clear Fork Station.

◇

When Mrs. Phillips awoke some hours later, she was greatly disappointed to find herself lying in a pool of her own blood with the Gates of Heaven nowhere in sight.

After taking stock of her condition she set about the task of removing the arrows from her body and dressing her own wounds.

She then struck out to walk three miles to her nearest neighbor's to seek help, to sound the alarm of the Indian attack, and to report the capture of the Miller women and the children.

Upon leaving her house Mrs. Phillips discovered the body of Rebecca Miller's babe lying in her side-yard with its brains dashed upon a stone. She returned into the house, brought a blanket and wrapping the body in it she returned to the house and placed the bundle in an empty dresser draw.

She then resumed her trek to her neighbors.

◇

Close to 9:00 A.M. the next morning Greg Hilliard, a cowboy who worked for the Swager Creek Outfit, tied his horse at the hitching post outside the saloon and came in with his body language expressing despair, "Gimme a whiskey Tee."

"Sure thing Greg," Tee replied.

Setting a glass on the bar before him, Tee remarked, "I'm surprised to see you here this early, and on a workday," as he poured a drink into the glass.

Looking Tee in the eye Greg said sternly, "This ain't a workday. I come to see if you gents will ride with us to chase down a band of Indians that attack a settlers place over on Lambs Head Creek yesterday evening."

"We can't both go. One of us has to stay here to mind the station," Tee observed.

"We ain't heard nothing about an Indian raid," Jim remarked. "What happened?"

Greg paused to take a sip of his drink, then said, "They was five Indians took two women and three children hostages, and they killed a baby by bashing its head on a tree trunk, and they shot the settlers wife twice with arrows and thinking she was dead they scalped her.

"She's a mighty tough woman. She lay there and pretended to be dead while that butcher scalped her.

"I think I'm a pretty tough hombre, but I don't reckon I could do that."

"I don't believe I could either," Tee admitted, while absent-mindedly wiping the bar with a towel.

"She living?" Jim asked.

"Yeah. After the Indians left, she bandaged her own wounds and then walked three miles to get help," Greg replied, and taking another sip of his drink he went on. "She's in pretty bad shape, but they think she'll pull through if infection don't set in."

"Who's riding with you?" Tee asked.

"They's a bunch of us making up a posse over at the Nail headquarters.

"They said to bring five days supplies, a good rifle, and an extra horse, if you can," Greg replied.

"Well, like I said, we can't both go," Tee commented.

"You go with 'em," Jim offered. "You're a better rider than me and a better shot too. I can handle the station alone for a few days."

"Alright," Tee responded, and turning to Greg, "I can bring a mule to pack on, if you want me to."

Tossing down the remainder of the drink, Greg agreed, "Yeah, bring your mule, and come on as soon as you can.

"I'm gonna ride on now. We'll leave a trail you can follow if we leave before you get there."

◇

The old cook at the Nail headquarters said the posse had been gone about an hour-and-a-half when Tee arrived.

"They went yonder," the old man said, pointing a weathered hand to the south. "Colonel Smith in charge."

"Colonel Smith, ay?"

"Yeah," the old man replied knowingly.

"Well, I guess I'd better make tracks if I'm gonna catch up to 'em," Tee offered as he pulled his pony around and spurred it into motion.

The old man watched him ride away without further comment. In a few moments he spat a charge of tobacco juice onto a nearby plant, and turned away to attend his own business.

◇

Tee didn't have any difficulty following the posse's trail. They were heading south, maybe a little east.

The trail meandered between the flat-toped mesas that were prevalent in the area and skirted scraggly dry washes that rambled off the mesas in arrays that eventually merged into dry creeks.

Eventually the trail left the mesa country behind and continued a little east of south into gently roiling hills that were covered with brick-red topsoil that supported denser vegetation than the semi-desert country around Clear Fork Station.

An hour before sundown Tee crossed Pecan Bayou.

I declare. These Texas folks sure have strange notions about naming their streams. That Clear Fork is anything but clear, and this shallow little stream don't come close to my notion of a bayou, Tee grumped to himself as he made the crossing.

The last twilight was fading in the west when Tee found the posse's camp located on a small creek.

When he was within shouting distance Tee called, "Hello the camp, Tee Wells here."

"Come on in," someone shouted back.

Greg Hilliard walked out a few steps to met Tee and when they met Greg took the reins of Tee's horse and held them while Tee dismounted.

"Glad to see you catch up," Greg offered as the two men started the task of unsaddling and then hobbling the horse and mule so that they could graze during the night.

"How many men do we have?" Tee asked.

"You make ten," Greg replied.

And continued, "The trackers figure they got about a days start on us, but they think we've made up two to four hours on 'em.

"We was all deputized by Colonel Smith before we left. Come on over by the fire and he'll give you a badge too, I expect."

"What are we deputies of?" Tee inquired.

"Colonel Smith. He was a Colonel in the Army of The Republic Of Texas" Greg replied.

"He don't hold any official office that I know of now," Tee argued.

"Well, the Colonel said if we had a badge that whatever we did would be legal and proper in the eyes of the state. So we all held up our hand and said, 'I do,' and got us a badge," Greg replied.

"I'll be over in a bit, I want to get my bedroll and belongings situated first," Tee delayed.

"Yeah, come on over, coffees ready now, supper 'ill be ready in a bit.

"Our cook from the S C O (the Swager Creek Outfit ranch brand) came with us, so we ought to have some pretty good eating," Greg concluded.

◇

Tee was setting on his heels drinking coffee, idly listening to the men talking among themselves, he knew most of the men in the posse from their having done business with the store and the saloon.

There was Bill James, a settler who had a place over on Stony Creek, Bob Dublin another settler from over that way, and Howdy Jones, and Cleve, and Greg.

And there was The Elder Williams, a Fundamental Baptist lay preacher who held prayer meetings where foot washing was part of the service, an idea that Tee found completely off-putting.

Tee learned from listing to the men talk that it was the wife of Ward Phillips' who had been shot with arrows and scalped, and that Ward and the Miller brothers were away on business when the attack took place.

The Miller brother's wives, along with their children, were visiting the Phillips place when the Indians attack.

The infant killed in the Phillips' front yard was the child of the younger Mrs. Miller and the five-year-old girl and seven-year-old boy belong to the other Miller woman while the six-year-old boy was the son of the Phillips'.

Tee observed two men coming into camp. One he recognized as Juan Martinez who was a well-known tracker in the area. He didn't know the other man.

If asked, Juan claimed he was Mexican, but the talk was that he was Indian.

Tee supposed that if Juan was Indian he would say so because it was well known by all that Texans despised Mexicans more than they did Indians.

The two men went directly to Colonel Smith with whom they had a whispered conversation, the animation of the three expressing anger and despair.

In a few moments Colonel Smith stepped to the center of the group and spoke gravely.

"The scouts have found the body of the younger woman who was taken captive about two hundred yards over to the east of us.

"It appears she was outraged by the heathen savages until she bled to death from her private parts.

"I'm asking for married men to volunteer to go wash her, and wrap her in blankets, and bring her back here where we will bury her.

"Some of you other boys can get started digging a grave while the married men are taking care of their duties," the Colonel directed.

The hard ground prevented the men from digging as deep a grave as they would have liked. While some men worked at digging others gathered stones to be placed over the mound of earth to protect the body from predators and to mark the grave more permanently than the wooden cross someone fashioned from tree limbs.

When the married men returned with the young woman's body wrapped head to toe in blankets, three lariats were laid on the ground at the foot of the grave parallel to each other perpendicular to the grave and the woman's body was laid upon them. Six men took up the ends of the lariats and in unison moved the body over the grave and gently lowered her into the ground.

All the posse men gathered around the grave with Colonel Smith standing near the head of the grave, the Colonel asked, "Does anyone know her name?"

"Rebecca Miller, she's the sister-in-law of the other woman captive," someone in the group answered.

"Elder Williams, will you say a few words over her?" the Colonel invited.

Elder Williams stepped to the head of the grave and removing his hat said, "Let us pray."

When all the men had removed their hats and bowed their heads the Elder commenced, "Our Father we pray your blessings be bestowed on our sister Rebecca who we bring before you having fallen victim to her untimely death at the hands of heathen savages. We ask, Oh Lord, that you receive her into Heaven and welcome her to your glory forever.

"We pray for forgiveness of our sins and for the sins of those who did this terrible thing to this our sister."

Colonel Smith popping to attention said angrily, "Elder, and all the rest of you, let me tell you now, if God forgives them savages that's his business but my business is sending them to his judgment, and to damnation I hope.

"I intend to hang 'em if I can get my hands on 'em, and if I can't I intend to shoot them down like dogs.

"If there's any of you men who aren't a hundred percent with me on that, then pack up and ride home now."

The Colonel waited a few seconds, and when no one spoke he announced, "Amen! You men fill that grave in and lets eat supper."

◇

By the time the men got to their supper the cook had prepared hours earlier, the steaks had turned dry and tough.

Tee thought the sole of his boot would have made a better meal.

Sharp stones scraped Tee's back where he lay on the ground rolled in his blanket, and the hatred for the Indians boiled in his heart and was reflected in the sourness of his stomach, all conspiring to render a mostly sleepless unrestful night.

In the morning the posse men were up early, saddled, and ready to ride as soon as it was light enough for the trackers to follow sign.

The Elder and the man Tee didn't recognize informed the Colonel that they were turning back.

"The Elder and one of his foot-washers turning tail," someone sneered.

The Colonel locked a stern glare on the man and said, "These men act out of conviction, not cowardice. I'll have no talk to the contrary!"

None of the men could hold the Colonel's stare.

◇

Charlie Paddlefoot dispatched Bat Ears to the top of a hill with instructions to watch for anyone coming after them.

Apprehensive at being left behind, Bat Ears asked, "How long should I watch?"

"If you see nothing by sunset today, come on to us. Tonight we will camp at the creek that is full of turtles at the big river the white men call Colorado."

It was half-an-hour before sundown when Bat Ears saw the dark mass move over a ridgeline far north of him.

He watched the mass intently until it disappeared from his view, mounted his pony and rode at a gallop to find his comrades.

Bat Ears reached the camp about an hour before sunup.

"Many men are coming." He told Charlie Paddlefoot excitedly.

"How many?"

"Maybe as many as all my fingers two times."

Marian Miller didn't understand the Comanche language, but she perceived that Bat Ears was saying as many as twenty men were coming after the savages.

She was so overwhelmed with hope that she lost control of her emotions and wept openly.

Eagle Claw scolded her in Comanche and raised his hand in preparation to strike her. Cowering away, she forced herself to be silent.

"This is a good place to kill 'em," Hawks asserted. "We will leave tracks into the creek for them to follow, and when there in line in the creek, we can kill 'em from the brush on its sides."

"They have the six shot pistols, and rifles. We will not kill half of them before they kill all of us," Charlie Paddlefoot argued.

"Did we not come to kill white men?" Hawks demanded.

"Yes. But I intend to kill more than one or two before they kill me. If you wish to die here, then stay, but I will not die here," Charlie Paddlefoot declared

◇

Thirty minutes before sundown of the second day the posse followed the Indians trail to a point where it led into the shallow waters of a small creek not far from its confluence with the Colorado River.

"What do you make of them sign, Colonel?" Juan asked.

After a moments thought the Colonel replied, "Well, three things come to mind right away.

"First is, they rode down that creek to gain access to the river so they could cross.

"Second thing is, they rode down that creek a ways and cut out where we'll have a hard time finding their trail, and the third thing is they're holed up in the brush waiting for us to ride into that narrow creek bottom where they can shoot us like shooting fish in a barrel."

Juan replied dryly, "Yeah, I expect that's about right."

"You ride down that creek and see if you can find out if they cut out or went into the river," the Colonel directed. "I'll have men ride on either side of the creek and watch for an ambush and for any trail they may have left if they didn't cross the river."

So deployed, the posse men carefully worked their way toward the riverbank arriving there safely after having traveled about three hundred yards.

Juan reported that he had seen sign that the Indians had entered the river, but he couldn't see a likely place for them to have exited on the other side.

"We'll make camp here for the night," the Colonel asserted. "I want one man to scout up the river for a place we can get out on the far side, and one man to scout downstream.

"You scouts can hunt for some fresh meat for supper while you're looking for a place to cross.

"I want four men to build a raft that we can float our tack and supplies across on, and I'll help the cook get coffee made and get the camp setup."

◇

One of the hunters brought in a young doe that was butchered and cooked as were a pot of beans and sourdough bread.

Tee thought these and coffee made a far better meal than the shoe-leather steak he had tried to eat the night before.

The downstream scout reported a creek entering the river on the far side about four hundred yards downstream and around a bend where the current was likely to push flotsam toward the creek's mouth but then sweep it away just before it reached the landing.

◇

In the morning while the posse was having breakfast before sunup, Colonel Smith laid out his plan for crossing the Colorado River.

"I want two men to go string a rope across the river with its far end terminating at the landing. That'll provide a hand line for anyone who doesn't make it to the landing.

"There's no telling how far down that river you would be taken before you could get out if you miss the landing, and it'd be a ride I don't expect you'd survive.

"When the rope is in place we'll start the raft with two men on it.

"When it is near the landing, if it looks like it may not make the landing on its own, you men on the bank throw ropes to the men on the raft and pull them in.

"When the raft is in, then the rest of us will start with the horses, and if we're having trouble making the landing then you men on the bank throw ropes to us to help us in."

The plan set, Howdy and Cleve were assigned the task of stringing the hand line across the river.

While they were about that duty, the raft was loaded and made ready to launch.

When the raft was away, the horses were tied in a loose string with ropes around their necks leading from one horse to the next.

While the men who were going to guide the horses across were waiting for the order to go, Greg said, "You know, I'm not all that good a swimmer. I think I'll find me a good dry log to hang onto while we make that swim."

"Well, get it done. We're going to be ready to go pretty quick," someone commented.

Tee observed, "The current don't look near as strong next to the far bank as it does in the middle of the river, so lets work our way over next to that far bank and maybe we'll find some places where the water will be shallow enough that we won't have to swim all the way down to the landing.

"Yes, lets try that," Colonel Smith agreed. "I'm not all that strong a swimmer myself, and that landing is a mighty long way down the river."

◇

The crossing was made safely in a few minutes after which the packhorses and mules were loaded, the mounts were saddled, and the posse was on its way south by the time the sun was thirty minutes high.

During the third day on the trail, the country the posse was passing through slowly became rougher with more and more stone faced drainages, most of them dry, making the going difficult and slow.

The tracker was having trouble keeping to the trail the Indians had left in the rocks slowing the posse even more.

By late on the fourth day the posse was well into the Texas Hill Country where they crossed the Guadalupe River about half-an-hour before sundown.

Having crossed the river, Colonel Smith ordered the cook to prepare the evening meal and ordered the men not to unsaddle their horses.

When the men were gathered around the Colonel addressed them saying, "Men I expect all of you know we've been loosing ground on the Indians, and this country just gets rougher the further we go. If we keep on like we're going, we're going to loose 'em altogether.

"Juan and I figure they'll run for Tarpley Pass, and if they get into that country west of there it'll be nearly impossible to catch 'em.

"So I've decided to ride through the night and try to cut 'em off at Tarpley.

"If we can pen 'em there, maybe we can negotiate the release of the hostages

"We'll ride as soon as we tend the stock and get ourselves a bite to eat."

◇

The first hint of gray was showing in the east when the posse spotted the craggy outline of Tarpley Pass standing about a mile away, outlined against the glow of stars.

The posse stopped, dismounted, and picketed their horses.

Colonel Smith spoke to the men, keeping his voice barely above a whisper, "I want you men to spared out and move in as quietly as possible. I don't want to spook 'em before we're in close range of 'em, and be exceptionally careful where you shoot. Don't shoot unless you have a certain target. None of us want to shoot one of the children."

"Do you know they're in there?" someone asked.

"No, but we're going to act like they are until we know different."

The posse had reached a point about thirty yards from the base of the pass when the light was good enough to see the Indians getting ready to mount their ponies.

Juan fired the first shot, killing one of the ponies that an Indian had just vaulted onto dumping the Indian out of sight behind a boulder.

In the next few seconds the Indians seemed to have been thrown into a state of confusion with their ponies kicking and bucking and trying to escape. The Indians were whooping and shouting, and scurrying for cover.

The posse fired a strong volley into the Indians camp, and finally some of the Indians began to return arrows in the direction of the posse.

The Indians soon were able to get their ponies into the shelter of boulders and in a few more minutes the firing on both sides trailed off to an occasional pot-shot by one side or the other.

As the day wore on, the Indians began a campaign of springing up from behind their cover, loosing an arrow at the posse, and quickly dropping back below their cover.

The posse men returned fire each time, but the Indians were out of harms way long before the rifle bullets reached them.

Taking aim at a spot where an Indian had stood and loosed an arrow, Tee waited.

Nearly an hour had passed before an Indian sprang up in the spot where Tee's rifle was aimed.

He squeezed the trigger.

An instant later the Indian was knocked backward by the impact of Tee's bullet striking his upper chest. The Indian let out a whoop intended to be intimidating, but was tempered with pain.

The Indians then changed their tactic to shooting arrows high into the sky and having them rain in on the posse men where they lay in shallow drainages or crouched behind boulders.

It soon became clear that the Indian's original tactic had been used to gain knowledge of the posse men's locations thereby giving the Indians specific targets and forcing the posse men to move to new locations.

While moving, some of the men exposed themselves to direct attacks from the arrow shooting Indians, and one man received a minor leg wound.

◇

With neither side able to gain a distinct advantage by mid afternoon it became obvious that after sundown the Indians could make good their escape thereby leaving the posse hours in their wake.

Colonel Smith asked Juan and Howdy to try to flank the Indians' position thereby catching them in a crossfire.

Juan and Howdy reasoned that the terrain to the south of their position looked more penetrable than did that to the north, so they traveled about a mile south before they tried to scale the escarpment.

Finding the face of the cliff littered with loose rock that easily shifted and fell taking more rocks and dirt with them, and some hiding rattlesnake dens, the climb proved to be difficult, dangerous, and to take far longer to accomplish than the men had anticipated.

When they were finally on top, the men found themselves on a flat mesa that extended as far as they could see to the northwest and to the southeast, and they were surprised by how near sundown the hour had become.

Looking about, Howdy commented, "If that was the easy up, I'm damned sure glad we didn't take the hard way."

"I'm not sure we would have made it if it had been any harder," Juan replied.

The men hurried along the mesa in the direction of the Indian's encampment. When they arrived at a point where they imagined that they could look directly down on the Indians, they crept to the edge of the escarpment and peeked down.

The men saw Marian Miller setting on the ground, her back resting against a boulder, her feet extended in front of her. She held the three children clutched close to her.

She immediately saw the men looking down at her and reacted with terror sweeping her face. She hugged the children even closer to her.

Her reaction gave away Howdy and Juan's position thereby warning the Indians of their presence. Neither man was able to get a clear shot at the Indians before they were under cover.

After a few moments Marian Miller lowered her gaze to contemplate her feet, while still holding the children close about her.

◇

Shortly after sundown, when there was no moon, there was starlight on the mesa leaving the depths of the pass extremely dark; Howdy and Juan heard the Indians moving through the pass.

They didn't fire at the sound of the Indians departing for fear of hitting one of the hostages. Instead, they ran for the head of the pass hoping to cutoff the Indians retreat but arrived too late and although they could see the Indians departing, they never had an identifiable target to fire upon.

The men returned to the posse stumbling and falling their way through the dark pass. They arrived a little before midnight to inform Colonel Smith that the Indians were hours gone.

"You men take some rest," the Colonel directed. And to the cook he said, "Lets have breakfast done with thirty minutes before sunup."

◇

While the men sat on their heels around the breakfast campfire the Colonel confided, "When we catch them Indians I'll take the responsibility of doing what has to be done with the woman. I won't put that off on any of you."

"Well Colonel," Tee said sternly, "back yonder when you made clear what you intended for the Indians I didn't get the drift that you intended the same for the woman or I'd have turned back with the Elder."

"She's been with them bucks for six nights," the Colonel argued, "there ain't nothing else to do with her."

"I won't be going any further with you Colonel, "Tee replied firmly. "I'm turning back here."

"I hope you don't mind if we keep your pack mule," the Colonel growled. "But it really don't make a tinkers-dam if you do, I'm keeping it anyway."

Tee waved his hand in resignation, saying, "Keep it."

◇

When breakfast was finished the Colonel ordered Juan and Greg to have a look in the rocks where the Indians had been hidden during the day before to determine whether or not any harm had been done to them.

"I'd like to go along with 'em," Tee said. "I think I hit one of 'em pretty good yesterday, and I'd like to see for myself."

"You and Juan go, Greg can stay here and help pack up the camp," the Colonel agreed.

When Juan and Tee came near the rocks where the Indians had been hold up, Juan signaled for Tee to stop and remain quite.

Juan drew his pistol, holding it in front of himself at about waist level, he whispered to Tee that he had heard some noise from behind the boulder immediately in front of them.

The men crept around the boulder, their guns ready to fire at an instants notice.

When Tee cleared the boulder and could see what was in back of it he first thought he had found a bundle of rags.

In a moment the bundle moved and his vision resolved, revealing two children, cowering, huddled with their arms around each other.

Juan saw the children in almost the same moment and exclaimed, "They left the children! I can't believe my eyes, they left the children."

"The two smaller ones, it appears," Tee observed.

Holstering his pistol and setting on his heels, Tee asked, "Are you buttons aright?"

The children stared, their eyes wide and fearful, they didn't move, and didn't. answer.

"You don't need to be afraid of me," Tee said gently. "Me and these other men have come to take you home."

Juan shouted to the Colonel and beckoned for him and the others to come to the boulders.

When the posse men were near Juan said, "Colonel the Indians left the two smaller children here."

"I sure didn't expect that," the Colonel admitted.

"Why do you think they would do a thing like that?" someone in the posse asked.

"To slow us down, I suppose," someone else replied.

The men marveled at the children, approaching carefully, offering food and water, trying awkwardly to comfort the tots.

In a few minutes Juan reported he had found one dead Indian, apparently the one Tee had shot, and one dead horse, apparently the one he had shot.

"It appears the woman and older boy are still with the Indians," he concluded.

"We had better get riding," the Colonel ordered. "Taking these two buttons is going to slow us down so much we may never catch 'em."

"No need to take 'em with you," Tee offered. "I'll take 'em with me."

"You can't take those children back over that country we came over. You'll all be killed if you try," the Colonel observed.

"I expect you're right about that," Tee agreed. "I was thinking I'd try to find a settlement hereabouts where I could get some help, but I don't know this country so I don't know exactly where to look, but I reckon we aren't too far from San Antonia."

"It's about fifty miles southeast to San Antonio," Juan offered. "But about twelve miles due east is Bandera. It's a settlement of Polish immigrants. The Polish are kind people, and they'll help you. If I were you, I'd take the children to the Father at the Catholic Church. He'll know who speaks English and who is most able to help."

◇

Tee and the children remained in the vicinity of Tarpley Pass for the remainder of that day.

Tee killed two rabbits and made a stew of them and he and the children ate and rested, the children sleeping until mid afternoon.

When they awoke he fed them more rabbit stew.

The children having now lost their fear of him, and being energized by their rest and food, the trio removed their shoos and stockings and frolicked in the cool, clear, water of the shallow creek beside which they were camped.

There was an instant when the girl's head was tilted a little to the right, her hair was flying free, her blue eyes sparkled above a mischievous smile while she splashed water on the boy, that Tee saw Lela in her and wished that the children were his and Lela's.

In the next moment Tee was filled with regret at what might have been. He sat on the creek-bank dangling his feet in the cool water while watching the children play, but he didn't rejoin them in their frolic.

When the novelty of the play wore off it was near sundown. The trio returned to their camp, ate the remainder of the rabbit stew, and fell asleep, sleeping peacefully through the night.

◇

In the morning Tee put the children on his horse. He walked and led the horse, coming to Bandera about two hours before sundown He went to St. Stanislaus Church where he surrendered the children to Sister Mary Elizabeth who placed them with a kind family with children of the same age where they would be safe and well cared for until their relatives could retrieve them.

◇

The following day Tee arranged transportation for himself back to Clear Fork Station.

He left Bandera before noon taking with him letters from Sister Mary Elizabeth addressed to the children's family, should he be able to locate them.

◇

Sixteen days after he left to join the posse Tee stepped off the westbound mail wagon at Clear Fork Station.

Jim was busy helping hitch the mule team to the wagon so didn't at first notice him.

When Jim finally looked up from his work he called, "Ha, look who's home. I'm sure glad to see you back here. It turns out there's a lot more work to do around here than I want to do by myself."

"Glad to be back. You got any coffee on in there?" Tee asked, hooking his thumb toward the house.

"Sure," Jim replied. "I'll be in as soon as I get rid of this here muleskinner and get this team he's wore out in the corral."

Tee was sitting at one of the card tables in the saloon sipping on a cup of coffee and smoking a cigarette when Jim came in from the corral.

"You-all catch them Indians?" Jim asked, while he poured himself a cup of coffee and joined Tee at the table.

"Well, we did, and we didn't," Tee began.

He went on to tell Jim all the details of the chase, and the firefight at Tarpley Pass and his taking the children to Bandera while the rest of the posse went on after the Indians and their captives.

Jim added, "The Miller brothers took off two days after you left to try and catch up to the posse, and to find their women folks and their kids."

"All that one of 'em will find is his woman's grave, and if Colonel Smith has his way that's what the other one will find too," Tee replied, tossing his cigarette stub into the spittoon that sat beside the table.

After taking a sip of coffee from his tin cup, Jim commented, "Ward Phillips stayed home to tend his wife. She's still in pretty bad shape."

"I found her scalp on the body of that Indian boy I killed at Tarpley Pass," Tee confessed grimly. "I buried it there."

Jim studied the beams of sunlight coming through the door and took a sip of his coffee.

After a moments silence Tee, seeming to think aloud said, "I can't puzzle out whether it would be a comfort to her to know that or not."

Jim replied apologizetly, "I don't recon I can be any help to you in that matter."

"The boy I took to Bandera was the Phillips child. The girl is the child of the woman that the Indians still have," said Tee.

Jim thoughtfully loaded his pipe, lit it, and took a slow drag.

"Well, it's too bad either way. If Colonel Smith catches 'em or if he don't," Jim concluded.

After a few moments of silence, while both men sipped their coffee, Tee changed the subject; "I got some bad news while I was waiting on the westbound mail wagon in Jacksboro."

Jim looked at him questioningly.

"The sheriff told me John Simpson is in this country asking questions about the killing of Thad."

"I was in hopes that he wouldn't come," Jim offered.

"I was too," Tee replied, looking into the distance, at nothing, "I sure hate the notion of killing another man."

"I've just now got to where I can sleep the night through, one or two nights a month, without dreaming about shooting Thad."

Still looking in the distance, Tee went on, "In the dream I can see the shot fly out of the gun and into his chest, and I can see them shot inside him ripping him apart like pack of wolves on a downed calf, and the look on his face knowing he's killed, and his eyes damning me to hell for the doing of it. I'll bet I've dreamed that a thousand times, and killing that boy at Tarpley Pass didn't help none either."

Looking at Jim now, Tee said earnestly, "Yes sir, I sure hope I don't ever have to kill another man."

◇

Late in the afternoon on the Saturday after Tee had arrived home, Howdy Jones burst into the saloon calling, "Tee, gimme a whiskey. I'm dryer than a bone in a peach orchard."

Tee sat a glass on the bar and pouring a generous drink, asked, "You gents all make it back home alright?"

"Oh yeah, we're all finally back," Howdy replied, lifting the glass, taking a sip.

"Did ye' catch them Indians?"

"Naw. Never seen them again after we left Tarpley Pass," Howdy said, shaking his head in the negative.

"I tell you Tee, if you think that country we went through getting to Tarpley Pass was bad you hadn't seen the half of it compared to what was west of there."

Howdy took another swallow of his drink, and went on, "It weren't nothing but one rock cliff after another for the next hundred miles, and if we were following a trail I sure couldn't see any sign of it, but Colonel and Juan said we was, so we kept on."

Howdy finished his drink, and gestured for Tee to pour another as he continued.

"We finally broke out of that rock country and went down into a pure-de desert. Every thing in it had a thorn or a stinger and every damned one of 'em got me. There wasn't a square inch of my hide that wasn't stabbed, or stung or scratched, or bit."

Howdy leaned his left elbow on the bar, shifted his weight to his left foot, and picking up the glass with his right hand took a good swallow of the whiskey before he continued.

"By the time we finally come to the Devils River our horses was give out, and so was we.

"But I tell ye that Devils River was a fine thing to see. Clear cool water flowing over smooth round rocks, and I declare it was so full of fish it looked like you could walk across on their backs."

"Howdy, how full of fish was that river?" Jim asked, grinning.

"You asked Greg when he gets here if you don't believe me."

"Oh, I believe you Howdy, I surely do" Jim teased.

Tee mechanically wiped the bar with his towel while Howdy took another swallow before he continued.

"Our horses was so give out that we had to leave 'em, and every thing else we didn't want to carry on a forty mile walk to Sonora.

"At Sonora we got ourselves a ride with a freight outfit headed to Fort McKavett, and from there we got rides with Army wagons from one place to another till we worked our way back home."

"Well, Howdy, I don't believe I'm much disappointed that I missed that part of that ride," Tee asserted.

"I'm damned if I'd been disappointed to have missed it myself," Howdy declared.

◇

Men drifted in one or two at a time until the saloon had the best crowd it had ever had, and for the first time in the history of Clear Fork Station there wasn't a single conversation concerning beef prices, screwworms, or rain.

All the conversation dwelled on the misfortune of the Miller and Phillips families, Indian depredations, and Colonel Smith's posse.

About ten-thirty in the evening a stranger wearing a cross-draw rig, dressed in slouchy clothing, and sporting a scruffy beard stepped through the saloon doors.

Tee was behind the bar and Jim was standing in front of the bar a little to Tee's right when the stranger stopped a step inside the saloon doors and called in a loud voice, "Which one of you suns of a bitch is Wells?"

All conversation stopped. Every eye in the saloon turned to look at the intruder.

Tee recognized John Simpson immediately. Except for being an inch shorter than Thad, he was an exact copy.

Turning with all others to face the stranger Jim announced, "I'm Jim Wells."

"I'm the one you've come for Simpson. Leave him be," Tee ordered.

"You the back-shooting bastard killed my brother?"

"Me and Thad shot one-another. Neither in the back."

"I've come to kill you, so fill your hand."

"I've got a twelve-gage leveled on your middle under this bar, so you unbuckle that pistol and let it drop. Another killing won't bring your brother back."

"You burn in hell."

Tee saw Simpson's hand grip his pistol's butt and knew that he should shoot, but he did not shoot.

He saw Simpson pulling the pistol out of its holster and he knew that he should shoot, but he did not shoot.

Tee saw Simpson thumbing the hammer back as he drew the pistol clear of the holster and he knew that he should shoot, but he did not shoot.

He saw Simpson swing the muzzle of the pistol around to bear on him and he knew that he should shoot, but he did not shoot.

Tee saw smoke and flame explode from the pistol's muzzle and he knew that he should shoot, but he did not shoot.

In his peripheral vision, Tee saw Jim flinch, and in his central vision he saw Simpson thumbing the hammer on his pistol for a second shot.

Tee pulled the triggers on the twelve-gage. The shot load sent Simpson reeling backward through the saloon doors and onto the gallery where he fell on his back, the life gone from his eyes.

Tee sprang around the bar to where Jim had crumpled to the floor with copious amounts of blood pulsing from a wound in the interior of his right leg about halfway between the knee and the groin.

"We gotta get that blood stopped." Tee observed. "There's fire in the cook stove in yonder. Somebody get an iron red hot."

"I'll get it," someone in the crowd volunteered.

"We gotta do something quicker than that," someone else asserted. "We need to get a strap around his leg above that wound and pinch that blood flow off."

A strap appeared and was applied. The blood flow slowed, but wasn't stopped.

Jim's eyes were glassy, and he looked lost. Finally he focused on Tee and said accusingly, "You's gonna let him shoot you. Wasn't ye'?"

"I didn't want to kill another man Jim, but I sure am sorry as hell I let him shoot you."

"Well, what's done is done, and we're both still here."

"Yeah, we're both still here."

When the red-hot iron was brought, Jim was given a thick piece of leather to place between his teeth while the iron was applied to the wound.

When the deed was done the bleeding was stopped and Jim, lay unconscious.

"I seen a man wounded like that in the Mexican War, and they had to take his leg off on account of there ain't no blood going past the wound," Greg Hilliard stated.

"Yeah, I'm gonna need to get him to a doctor as soon as I can," Tee answered.

"I'll hitch a team for you," Howdy offered. "You change teams at Franz's Station" (the Butterfield Overland Mail relay station halfway between Clear Fork Station and Fort Belknap) "and you ought to make Belknap in three hours, and the Army doctor there may help you, if he's there, and if he ain't there, or won't help, change teams at Belknap and again at Murphy's Station" (the Butterfield Overland Mail relay station halfway between Fort Belknap and Jacksboro) "and you ought to make Jacksboro in eight or ten hours."

◇

Tee made Fort Belknap at a quarter-to-two. He had the sentry roust the post surgeon who came to the wagon and taking a look at Jim's wound, said, "That leg is going to have to come off, Mister, and I can't treat civilians, so you need to go on to Jacksboro and see Doctor Brown over there. But there is something I can do, so wait here till I come back."

The doctor returned in a few minutes with a flask and a tablespoon. He gave Jim two tablespoons full of the dark amber liquid from the flask, and handed the flask and spoon to Tee, saying, "Give him a spoonful every two hours till you get to the doctor in Jacksboro"

"Whisky?" Tee asked.

"Laudanum."

"Ain't that habit forming?"

"Sure as hell is, but that's all I have to relieve the pain he's in."

Tee offered to pay the doctor who declined so he thanked him and headed for Murphy's Station, leaving Fort Belknap a little after two in the morning.

◇

Getting directions to Doctor Brown's office from a passerby on the streets of Jacksboro, Tee arrived a little after nine-thirty in the morning only to learn that Doctor Brown had gone to the settlement of Wizard Wells, about fifteen miles away, to deliver a baby and wasn't expected back until late in the day, or possibly not until tomorrow.

The doctor's wife, a woman in her late thirties or early forties that Tee didn't find especially attractive and whom, to Tee's way of thinking, displayed an overly assertive attitude, helped Tee get Jim into the doctor's office and made him as comfortable as possible.

She brought a bowl of broth and was able to get Jim to take about a cup full, and she got him to drink a small amount of water.

Tee sat with Jim and every two hours gave him a tablespoon full of Laudanum. The doctor's wife looked in often and brought coffee for Tee and tried to get Jim to take more broth and water, but had little success.

Eventually Tee began to observe his surroundings. On one wall of the doctor's office was a bookcase that extended from floor to ceiling. The bookcase was filled with books, most of them thick, bound, some in red, some in green, and some in brown. The titles were made up of mostly long words Tee couldn't begin to pronounce, so he supposed they were in some foreign language that only doctors understood.

On another wall was a cabinet filled with bottles, beakers, and flasks, some had powders in them, some had tablets or pills, and others had liquids of various colors. All of their labels bore words that Tee concluded must have come from the books in doctor's language.

On yet another wall sat a cabinet full of tools that only Satan would have known how to use. Tee wondered which of these the doctor would use to remove Jim's leg.

◇

At about one thirty in the morning the doctor returned home. He looked at Jim's wound and asserted that the leg would have to come off. But he was exhausted and the light from the lamps in the room didn't provide sufficient light for surgery, so he would perform the surgery in the morning.

He promptly went to bed leaving Tee to administer the Laudanum every two hours until morning.

A little before nine the doctor came into the room and while examining Jim's wound addressed Tee, "I want you to go to the Widow Chase's house and arrange for her to rent this man a room. My wife will give you directions of how to find the widow's place.

"Tell Mrs. Chase that your brother will be there at least a month, maybe two.

"When you get that done, go on to a café and have something to eat, or go to a saloon and get drunk if you please, but whatever you do don't come back here before one o'clock."

"Is he gonna be alright?" Tee asked tentatively.

"No he's not going to be alright," the doctor replied sharply. "I'm going to cut his leg off. He's not ever going to be alright again.

"Now go on about your business so I can get started."

<>

The Chase house was a white frame bungalow that sported two front doors that opened onto a covered gallery.

Tee could see that the right-hand door was partially blocked by a porch-swing that creaked softly on its chains as it swayed tentatively in the light morning breeze.

A path outlined with small stones, running from the street to the three steps that accessed the porch, addressed the left-hand door. The path was flanked by well-tended flowerbeds on each side, and was as clean as if it had been swept with a broom.

Tee rapped his knuckles on the doorframe of the left-hand door and waited patiently.

In less than a minute the door was opened by a slender, somewhat attractive middle-aged woman of medium height who had a narrow face, dark hair, brown eyes, and a strong chin.

"Yes?" she said. With the questions of who are you? And what do you want here? showing in her face.

"I'm Tee Wells, and Doctor Brown sent me here to inquire about renting a room for my brother."

"What's wrong with your brother?"

"Doctor Brown is taking off his right leg above the knee."

"Hu, an invalid. What happened to his leg?"

"He took a bullet that was intended for me."

"I don't want no renter in here that somebody's gunning for. Lord knows I've got enough trouble as it is."

"Nobody's gunning for him. He was gunning for me and I killed him."

"I heard there was a killing out at Clear Fork Station the day before yesterday. Was that you?"

"Yes ma'am."

"I don't approve of killing, nor killers," Maggie stated.

"No ma'am, I don't approve of killing either," Tee replied. "I'm the one that done the killing. My brother took a stray bullet that was intended for me. He's the one who needs the room. I won't be staying here."

"I usually charge four dollars a week for room and board and one bath a week and one change of linens a week, but I'm going to charge you ten dollars a week for taking care of an invalid and when he's able to do for himself I'll drop it to six dollars a week."

"Yes ma'am."

"You want' a see the room?"

"Yes ma'am."

Maggie stepped aside and gestured for Tee to follow her into the house.

Tee removed his hat as he entered her house and followed her to a bedroom that opened off the living room.

The room was small with one window. It was furnished with a small plain table, a narrow bed, and a straight-backed chair.

"I expect this'll do fine," Tee remarked.

"I won't have no drinking, cussing, smoking, or spitting in my house," Maggie asserted.

"Yes ma'am. I'll tell my brother."

"I'll tell him myself. And I'll see to it that he remembers it too. You see to it that you remember it if you visit here."

"Yes ma'am."

Tee thought as he headed for a café, *"Damned glad I'm not the one who's going to have to stay here a month or two."*

◇

The doctor ordered complete bed rest for the first ten days Jim was at Mrs. Chase's house.

Doctor's orders not withstanding, Jim insisted on hauling himself up to use a chamber pot as opposed to using a bedpan, which he thought to be the most barbaric notion he had ever heard.

After the tenth day Jim began learning to use crutches to get himself about and was soon able to make his way to the dining table for meals.

On the fourteenth day Maggie came-by a mess of black-eyed peas that needed to be shelled.

Jim had long since learned that Maggie liked to talk, and that she did so continuously.

Thinking that if he volunteered to shell the peas, and took them out to the porch swing to do the shelling, that Maggie would likely find something to do in the house.

This maneuver would, he thought, give him a break from her constant chatter, and it would be the first time he'd been out of the house in two weeks.

"I'll shell them peas for you," Jim said. "I can make my way out to the porch swing, and if you'll bring 'em out to me I'll set out there and do the shelling."

"Well, thank you," she said. "Go ahead on out there and I'll bring 'em."

She brought the bag of peas, and a bowl to put them in, and a receptacle for the cast-off shells, and returned into the house.

Jim breathed a sigh of relief only to find a second later that she was returning with a chair, which she sat nearby, and took her seat.

"Right after I turned sixteen," she began, "a neighbor of ours was having a barn-dance and my daddy bought me a new pair of shoes to wear to that dance.

"When I got there I was introduced to William Chase. He was a strapping young man, and handsome, I thought, and me and him danced the whole night till I wore holes in both of them new shoes.

"Just before daylight me and him walked out into the dark and he took me in his arms and he kissed me."

Maggie giggled self-consciously, and went on, "He did a right good job of it too, I might say."

Regaining her composure she continued, "Well, he ask me to marry him, and I said he'd have to ask my daddy."

"Before Mr. Chase came to see my daddy, I told him he was coming and what for."

"My daddy pitched a fit. He'd run him off with a gun, he said," Maggie smiled at the memory.

"I told my daddy my mind was made up and if he ran Mr. Chase off I'm gonna run off with 'em. Well, he pitched another fit at that, but in the end he gave in to me and we had a right nice wedding," Maggie looked pleased at this memory.

"I married Mr. Chase when I was sixteen, and his father gave us a hundred-and-sixty acre farm in Christian County Kentucky, and pretty soon we had four boys."

Jim nodded an acknowledgement, and shelled peas.

"You ever been to Christian County Kentucky, Mr. Wells?"

"No Ma'am, I'm afraid not."

"Well, it's a beautiful country. There's hills and trees and streams, and we had as good a bottomland farm as ever there was.

"But, back in fifty (1850) when ever Tom, Dick, and Harry headed to California to look for gold, Mr. Chase didn't let his shirt-tail hit 'em till we was on the road to California."

"There was a lot of 'em went," Jim commented, and busied himself with the peas.

"We crossed the Mississippi on a ferry at Cairo, Illinois."

"My brother was in Cairo, Illinois in eighteen-fifty," Jim interrupted. "He was courting a woman there, Lela Atkins."

"They marry?" Maggie inquired.

"No. She married another. It broke Tee's heart. He's not over it yet, and I don't expect he's ever going to get over her. I don't think he wants to."

"Sometimes it takes a long time to get over loosing someone you love," Maggie offered. "I've been a widow over eight years now, and sometimes when a shadow passes the window, or the house makes a noise, I still look, expecting to see Mr. Chase, and I'm real disappointed when he ain't there."

Maggie looked off into the distance for a moment before she continued her story.

"From Cairo we went on to Fort Smith and crossed the Arkansas on the Government ferry. From there we took the Butterfield Road, back then they called it the California Road, and we come on here to Jacksboro.

"When we got here Mr. Chase took the mules to the blacksmith to get 'em shoed and while he was doing that he stepped on a horseshoe nail that went right through his boot into his foot"

Jim gave her a look of acknowledgement, and went on with his work.

"Them boots was as wore out as everything else we had, including all of us," Maggie went on. "Anyway, he took the lockjaw (Tetanus) from it and his jaws locked just like they say. So, he couldn't take any food, and not much water, and then his muscles all went to cramping, and all the other bone joints froze.

"So, there he was with his head thrown back as far as he could, and his back arched, and his legs pulled back to match his head, and he lay that way suffering the agony of hell for three weeks before he finally died.

"In the old countries they called it the Screaming Death, and it surely was that for him."

"I'm sorry," Jim said with a tone of sincerity.

"Well, there I was, in the middle of nowhere with four half-grown boys and no idea of what I was gonna do next. Back then this town wasn't nothing but a bunch of saloons, gambling dens, and sporting houses. There wasn't no way for a decent woman to make a living.

"But, the preacher that done Mr. Chase' funeral took pity on me and told me that Mr. Dodson who had a right nice café out on the Butterfield road needed a cook.

"So, I went and seen him and he hired me and I cooked for that café sixteen hours a day for seven years."

Jim complemented, "I've been admiring your cooking ever since I've been here, even when I didn't have no appetite for anything. Now I can see why you're so good at it."

"I've sure enough had plenty of practice," Maggie smiled.

"Mr. Dodson didn't allow drunks or sporting women in his place, so one-day in the spring of fifty-eight (1858) there was a drunk cowboy come in the café and when Mr. Dodson went to put him out the cowboy shot him dead.

"Mr. Dodson was a well liked man in town by then, and the good men of this town hung that fool before he had time to sober up."

"Justice can be mighty quick in this country sometimes," Jim offered.

"Right after I went to work for Mr. Dodson I found out he had this house for sale and I made a deal with him that I'd work for half wages if he would put the other half toward paying for this house."

"Well, he agreed to it, but I didn't have the house nowhere near paid for when he got killed, but he had it in his will that if anything happened to him the house would be mine free and clear.

"Well, that caused talk all over town that me and him was carrying on with one another, but it wasn't so. He couldn't have treated me any more respectfully if I'd been his mother."

Jim said, "There's always people who have something to say about things they don't know anything about."

A HANDFUL OF STARS

"Regardless of what people say about me, I sure am grateful to Mr. Dodson for what he did for me. I don't know what would have become of me if hadn't been for him."

Seeing that Jim had finished the pea shelling, Maggie said, "I guess I'd better get them peas on to cook."

She rose and collected the bowl of peas from Jim and gathered the chair, and turning to look across the country she said, "You know when I was living in Kentucky I wanted to live in a country where I could see forever, and now that I'm here there ain't a blessed thing to see."

"It's a mighty bare country alright," Jim replied. "There are some craggy old hills over around Clear Fork Station, but no trees of course."

"I guess I'd better get these peas on," she said as she started into the house.

"I think I'll set out here awhile," Jim replied. "It's mighty pleasant out here today."

Jim sat in the swing and studied the country, and enjoyed the breeze, and reflected on Maggie's tale of how she came to be living in Jacksboro.

After awhile he wanted to go into the house where she was.

It struck Jim as odd that he would want to go in so soon where he knew she would chatter away at him. It was pleasant sitting in the swing, and he hadn't been out of the house in two weeks.

Over the next four weeks Maggie told Jim about her sons, one gone to the Army, one to sea, one back to Kentucky, and one to no one knew where.

She told him about her hopes, her dreams, and her fears, and he listened and nodded, and grunted, and said little.

◇

Six weeks after Tee had taken Jim to the doctor he was surprised to see Jim manage to get himself down off the mail wagon unaided, except for the crutches he used under each arm, and to swing-walk himself at a brisk pace from the wagon to the saloon door.

Jim turned at the door and called, "What was that old Howdy said? I'm dryer than a peach orchard boar? No, I'm dryer than a bone in a peach orchard. Well, whatever it was, I've been saving up for six weeks, so let's have a drink."

"Go ahead, I'll be there as soon as I'm done with this mail wagon," Tee replied.

Tee dreaded the moment of Jim's homecoming, fearing that he would direct his anger over having lost his leg toward him. Tee knew of a certainty that he could have, should have, stopped Simpson before he shot Jim's leg off.

Jim was seated at one of the card tables in the saloon when Tee came in, took a glass from behind the bar, pulled up a chair and sat down at the table with Jim.

Pouring a drink for himself, Tee said, "I'm pleased to see you in such good spirits. I was afraid you'd be mighty melancholy after all that you've been through."

Jim responded, "There ain't no use crying over spilt milk I reckon," and took a swallow of his drink.

"We both know I could have stopped Simpson before he shot you."

"Don't trouble yourself over none of that. There's a lot of things we would all do different if we could do them over, but we can't, so all we can do is go on from here."

"Thank you Jim. I surely do appreciate your feeling that way about everything."

Tee raised his glass in a salute.

Jim raised his glass to meet Tee's and both men took a goodly swallow.

After a few moments of silence, Tee asked, "How'd you and the widow get along?"

"Oh, I declare, that is the talkin'est woman I was ever around. I swear, her tongue is loose on both ends."

"Never shut up a minute, day or night."

"I know ever detail of everything that ever happened to her, or that she saw happen, or she heard of happening, or she thought might happen from the beginning of time to the end of the world."

Tee shook his head in the negative, took a swallow of his drink, and commented, "I don't believe it would take six weeks of that to drive me crazy."

"Well, it about drove me crazy the first week or two, but then I kind'a got use to it, and by the end I had come to kind'a enjoy hearing her go on like she does."

Jim took a swallow of the whisky, and continued, "There was a lot of the time I didn't have no idea what she was saying, but I liked the sound of her voice. It was pleasing to me, kind'a like listening to the birds singing."

"Like the birds singing? I don't know what to say to that," Tee mused.

"Well yeah, kind of a musical sound about it, you know."

"No, I never was around no talking woman that the sound of her struck me as musical," Tee replied.

"Yeah, I'm gonna miss the sound of her talking, and there are other things I'm gonna miss about her too."

"Other things? What other things?"

"For one thing, she's a damned fine cook," Jim assured.

"As you know, I cook just enough to keep from starving, and sometimes I figure I might have been better off to have gone hungry," Tee admitted.

"Is there anything else you're gonna miss about being around her?" Tee probed.

"Well, me and her got around to pleasuring one another a time or two before I left," Jim confessed.

"Wy' Jim, you damned old rooster," Tee teased, lifting his glass in salute.

"You keep a civil tongue concerning Maggie!" Jim snapped.

Tee was taken by surprise by Jim's strong admonition.

Taking a moment to think through the forgoing conversation; Tee spoke in a serious tone, saying, "I didn't get the drift of this conversation until just now. Are you thinking on asking her to marry?"

"I don't know. Maybe I am. I don't know if I could make her a living hobbling around on crutches, and I don't know if she would have me if I did ask her to marry.

"I don't know why she would. She can probably do a lot better than me."

Tee took a drink from his glass and replied, "She hasn't done better, and as far as you making her a living, you can run the saloon and store well enough on crutches and I can take care of the Butterfield business. We'd all get along alright."

"I'm gonna think on it awhile before I make up my mind," Jim said thoughtfully. "It didn't take me long to get used to her, maybe it won't take long to get over missing her either."

◇

On a pleasant morning in the early fall of 1860, Tee and Jim having completed their morning chores and there being no customers for the store or saloon, seated themselves on the saloon's gallery. They sipped their coffee and each man lit himself a smoke. They enjoyed the smell of cool dry air, and the view of the changing color of the leaves on the few scrubby trees visible in the river bottom.

The men had been enjoying their respite for several minutes when Jim directed his gaze toward the east and observed, "There's a party of six riders coming yonder."

Tee made no answer, but studied the riders as they approached observing that the men were relatively well dressed and exceptionally well mounted for working cowboys.

When the riders were about forty yards away Tee announced, "That's Colonel Smith in the lead."

"Them others are all ranch-owners hereabouts too," Jim added.

The riders stopped their horses directly before Tee and Jim: all of them wearing somber expressions.

"Morning gents," Tee welcomed. "I declare, I don't believe we've ever had such a fine looking group of visitors here before. What can we do for you gents this morning?"

Colonel Smith growled, "Satisfy a little curiosity."

"Glad to, if I can," Tee replied.

"It looks like a small herd came through here late yesterday, or early this morning," the Colonel asserted, intending the remark as a question, and gesturing to the tracks left by the cattle.

"Yesterday evening, about an hour before sundown," Tee returned.

"Who was driving 'em?" one of the other ranchers asked.

"Wy it was Howdy and a couple of new boys I don't know very well, but I think I heard 'em called Bill and Heck."

"Say where they was taking 'em?" another rider chided.

"They said Colonel Smith here, had sold 'em to a new settler over north-west of here and they was delivering 'em over there," Tee answered honestly.

"I didn't sell 'em. They did," Colonel Smith snorted.

Giving Tee and Jim a sour look the men spurred their mounts into a gallop and thundered through the cut in the riverbank, through the shallow water in the river, and up the other side onto the plain where they followed the trail of the herd.

"Wy' they mean to hang them boys!" Jim asserted.

"Damnation! I expect you're right, and I went and told on Howdy. I wouldn't have done that for the world, but I didn't have no idea them boys was rustling," Tee said regretfully.

"I sure hope them boys have sense enough not to let them old codgers catch 'em, but I doubt it," Jim offered seriously.

"The Colonel don't have any compunction when it comes to killing. He had every intention of hanging them Indians if he'd caught 'em, and he meant to kill the Miller woman too, but I suppose he'd of shot her in the head instead of hanging her," Tee remarked.

◇

Around four in the afternoon Howdy, Bill, and Heck reined their ponies to a stop in front of the saloon, dismounted, and tied-up to the hitch-rail.

Howdy, followed by Bill and Heck came blustering into the saloon; Howdy calling, "Tee pour us a whisky, we've been working hard today."

"Like hell you have," Tee snarled. "You've been rustling cattle, and Colonel Smith and five other ranchers are on your trail with lynch-ropes in their hands."

Surprised by Tee's assertion, Howdy asked, "How'd they know it was us?"

"I told 'em," Tee confessed. "The Colonel asked who drove that herd through here and I told 'em.

"I hate it like hell that I told 'em, but I didn't have no idea you were rustling," Tee apologized.

"We'd better get going," Bill said and made a move toward the door.

"Howdy, why are you rustling cattle?" Tee asked. "You knew it'd come to a lynching when you started."

Howdy looked like a spanked child and answered, "It's for the money.

"It takes a lot of money to keep Roseanne smiling at me, and I just couldn't let her go.

"I know now why they call it falling in love. Because once you start it don't matter what kind of woman she is, or even if your gonna get lynched for it, there ain't a damned thing you can do but keep on falling."

"You'd better do something about it now," Tee admonished. "You boys better ride for the tall timber and never come back to this country again. Colonel Smith won't forget, and he sure as hell won't forgive."

From where he stood in the door looking along their back trail Bill called, "We gotta go. Them old mossbacks are coming yonder," and with that warning Bill sprang for his horse.

Howdy and Heck followed quickly. They swung into their saddles and spurred for the scrub-brush cover of the river bottom.

Colonel Smith and his party, seeing the men riding away, stopped their horses, dismounted, and five of the men knelt, each on his right knee putting his left foot forward. Each man shouldered his rifle and holding its fore-stock in his left hand he braced his left elbow on his left knee, and opened fire on the fleeing cowboys. The sixth man held the reins of all their horses.

Some of their shots whooped into the stonewalls of the store and saloon and ricocheted off with the eerie whine that only a lead bullet can make.

None of their shots found their mark and soon the three cowboys were lost from sight in the cover of the river bottom.

The vigilantes mounted their horses, rode through the river crossing and up to the saloon where they dismounted and followed Colonel Smith inside.

The Colonel stopped two-thirds of the way between the door and the bar and demanded, "Tee did you tell them boys we're after 'em?"

"I did, and I'm sorry as hell I told you who they were. If I'd known this morning what you were up to I wouldn't have told you who they were."

"You help a thief you're as guilty as he is!" Colonel Smith asserted.

Tee asked sarcastically, "You aim to lynch me too?"

"I will if I please," the Colonel snarled.

Tee retrieved the double barrel twelve-gauge shotgun from under the bar. With the cocking of its hammers echoing through the saloon, Tee said sternly, "You come on and get started, and we'll both be in hell before sundown."

"You can't kill all of us with that thing," the Colonel said angrily.

"I can sure as hell kill you and one more. So, which one of you men want to go to hell with me and the Colonel?"

The men stood staring at the business end of the twelve-gauge, and no one moved.

After a few seconds Tee ordered, "You men get on your way, and if you catch them boys don't you hang 'em, you take 'em to the sheriff and let the law deal with 'em."

"You tend to your own business and I'll tend to mine," Colonel Smith advised.

"If you men catch them boys, before you start lynching 'em, you best think on the fact that there will be five other witnesses to whatever you do," Tee reminded the vigilantes.

CHAPTER 5

The Civil War Years

On a crisp sunny morning Tee was busy checking inventory in the store while Jim laboriously swept out the saloon.

"There's a buggy coming yonder the other side of the crossing," Tee called.

Jim took a moment to look, and observed, "Don't see many like that out here."

"No, we don't," Tee agreed. "Likely a drummer I expect. I sure hate for them fellers to come all the way out here and then we don't buy nothing from 'em."

"Can't buy from all of 'em. We wouldn't have space to put it all," Jim observed.

In a few minutes the buggy came to a stop in front of the saloon and a short portly man dressed in a business suit and a bowler hat stepped from the buggy.

The man walked from the buggy to the saloon with a bouncing stride that Tee found amusing to the point that he almost laughed aloud.

The man stopped inside the saloon door and asked, "Are you men the Wells brothers?"

"I'm Jim, and this here is Tee," Jim said, gesturing toward Tee. "You a hat drummer, are ye?"

"No? No, I'm Lester Peterson. I'm Superintendent of Division Six[14] of The Butterfield Overland Mail Company."

"Pleased to meet you Mr. Peterson," Tee said. "What happened to Mike O'Donnell?"

"All that I was told is that he quit for another job."

"Well, come on in. The bar's open, or we have coffee if you please."

"Thank you gents, but I'm not here on pleasant business. I'm here to close you down."

"Close us down? Why?" Jim asked.

"Congress is fearful that there is going to be a war between the North and South, so they have amended the mail contract to require us to take a road out through Kansas. So, we'll be closing all the stations from Tipton, Missouri to somewhere out in New Mexico in the next month."

Jim drew a chair from near one of the card tables and took a seat, saying, "I'm sorry to heart that."

"I sure hate to loose the Butterfield business," Tee offered. "But, I suppose we'll be able to get by on what we make from the store and saloon."

"The buildings belong to the company," Peterson advised. "If you men want to stay here you'll need to buy the property."

"Buy it! We built it with our own hands!" Tee exclaimed.

"I'm sorry gents, buy it or be out before the end of May," Peterson asserted.

"Well, I will be damned. I will just be damned," Tee muttered.

◇

On February 2, 1861 Texas seceded from the Union. By the end of February all Federal troops were ordered out of Texas.

A HANDFUL OF STARS

Some of the Federal forts were manned by Texas Militia who were soon ordered into the Confederate Army and sent to fight in the battles of the east, thus leaving the frontier, and the people thereon, to the mercy of the Plaines Indians.

The settlers, realizing their vulnerability on the frontier, agreed among themselves to form fortified communities for their mutual protection.

One such community that formed about ten miles down the Clear Fork below Clear Fork Station was Fort Davis.[15]

◇

By the time Fort Davis was being organized Tee had had time to cool off enough to think rationally and judged that he and Jim should investigate the possibility of moving the store and saloon to Fort Davis.

To that end, on a fine spring morning in late March, Tee hitched a team to the wagon and he and Jim drove the ten miles down the river to Fort Davis.

They found Fort Davis to be a 300 by 375 foot compact community of twenty-five picket houses with mudded-straw roofs and one stone house in its center. The community was bisected by an east-west street and was enclosed with a low picket fence that Tee thought would let more arrows through than it kept out.

On their arrival they found about 125 residents living in Fort Davis and that Colonel Smith was the head of a committee of settlers whom he had appointed to govern the settlement, so in effect his word was law.

Colonel Smith informed Tee and Jim that they were welcome to reside in the fort but all purchased goods would be bought by a cooperative of all the residents and sold to individuals at cost.

The Elder Williams raised strong objections to the presence of a saloon in the fort, and was supported in his view by his followers, who quickly convinced Colonel Smith of the wisdom of their point of view.

In less than two hours Tee and Jim were on their way back to Clear Fork Station.

While Tee drove the wagon Jim finished a pipe and knocked the spent ashes out on the steel tier of the wheel nearest where he sat.

"It's pretty clear them folks don't want us in their fort," Jim observed wryly.

"No," Tee chuckled, "I don't believe they do. And, to tell you the truth, I'm just as glad because with Colonel Smith running things I don't want to be there anyway."

"Ah, neither do I. But what do you think we ought to do? We won't have any business with everybody moving into the fort, and we sure would make an easy target for any Indian that came around, "Jim reasoned.

There being no road the wagon jolted along slowly following the tracks it had made when the men were on their way to Fort Davis.

After a brief silence, Tee replied, "I've been thinking, we could move to Fort Belknap, but I expect with the solders gone that little ol' place is gonna dry up and blow away in no-time, so I reckon the next best bet is Jacksboro."

"Jacksboro?" Jim questioned. "They've got plenty of stores and saloons already."

"You got a better idea, I'm listening," Tee replied.

"I reckon I ain't," Jim admitted.

"Why don't we drive over there tomorrow and look it over?" Tee asked.

"Yeah. Maybe I can talk Maggie into cooking us a fine supper while we're there," Jim mulled.

"Yeah, maybe you can," Tee smiled.

A HANDFUL OF STARS

◇

Tee and Jim arrived in Jacksboro in mid afternoon after overnighting on the trail. They put their wagon in the wagon yard, left their mules at the livery, and went to a hotel where they took a room at the exorbitant rate of a dollar a night.

They each had a bath, shaved, and put on their clean clothes, then went to a café and had supper. After supper they went to a saloon where they found a low-stakes poker game where they sat in and played poker and drank until around midnight.

In the morning they had their breakfast and then went to see the president of the bank, Mr. Willie Parker, to inquire about renting a building that would be suitable for the store and saloon.

Mr. Parker was a rotund man of medium height, graying hair, and an obnoxious squeaky voice.

So damned tight he squeaks when he talks. I'll bet he squeaks when he walks too, Tee thought as he and Jim were seated before a large mahogany desk across from Mr. Parker.

After barely civil greetings Mr. Parker got straight to business, asking what the men wanted of him.

They explained they wanted to move their store and saloon operation from Clear Fork Station to Jacksboro and wanted to know if Mr. Parker knew of a suitable building they could rent.

He gave them directions to two possibilities, which they went to explore.

When they returned they had selected a building about a half block off the square on The Butterfield Road. The location was outside the sporting district, which suited Tee and Jim's purpose, as they had no intention of operating a gambling den or brothel.

◇

Over the next three weeks Jim stayed in Jacksboro preparing the store and saloon for opening while Tee made five trips back to Clear Fork Station hauling the inventory and their belongings to their new location.

On at least four occasions during this period Jim persuaded Maggie to make dinner for him.

On the first Monday in May they opened for business. There were only a few customers, but they were off to a better start than they had experienced at Clear Fork Station when they were open for three days before the first customer showed up.

On Friday of their first week Dr. Brown came in. "Mr. Wells how are you doing with the crutches?"

"I've learned to get along with 'em pretty good I think. I've learned I can carry small things in my hands and swing along on the crutches just holding 'em with my elbows," Jim bragged.

"That's very good," Dr. Brown replied. "I'm glad to see you living here in town now. I'd like to work with you. I have an idea I thank will be very beneficial to you.

"There's an expert wood carver here that I think can carve a prosthetic for you and with it you can have full use of your hands and arms.

"Of course you'll walk with a sever limp, but it'll be more natural than crutches."

"A peg-leg?" Jim questioned with a negative tone.

"No, not exactly," the doctor explained. "I have in mind having the man carve a socket in the prosthetics where your stump would fit into it and a foot on the lower end where you would wear a shoe or boot. With your trouser leg down it would look fairly natural and the effect of the foot would be to give you a more stable balance."

"I declare," Jim pondered. "I hadn't even thought about such a thing. As far as the looks are concerned, everyone knows I have one leg, so I don't care about looks. Hell, I wasn't all that good-looking when I had two legs."

"Well, you think it over," the doctor encouraged. "If you decide to go on with it come see me so I can make a molding of your stump for the wood carver to work with before we try to fit it to you.

"While you're thinking about this, consider too that this will take a long time and will involve a lot of pain. Your stump is very tender and will take considerable effort on your part to learn to use a prosthetic," the doctor cautioned.

"Thank you doctor. I'll let you know in a few days," Jim concluded.

◇

Jim decided to accept the doctor's offer so the wood carver was set to work. It took a little over a month before the prosthetic was ready for the first fitting.

In spite of the doctor's warnings, Jim was deeply disappointed with the result when he discovered he wasn't able to tolerate the pain of standing upright.

Jim did not give up. Over the next six months he slowly learned to walk with the prosthetic. At first he only took a step at a time with the aid of the crutches, eventually several steps without crutches, but never outdoors without the aid of at least one crutch.

While Jim was learning to use the prosthetic he and Maggie were seeing more and more of each other.

Tee thought Jim was putting himself through all the pain more to impress Maggie than for any other reason.

During this period the war in the east grew ever more violent, and the three months it had been predicted to last had long since passed with no end in sight.

With more and more men being pulled away to the war business in the store and saloon had declined to the point that the operation was barely breaking even.

◇

On an evening in early December when there was a threat of snow in the air Jim returned from Maggie's home and taking a seat at the bar said, "Tee why don't you pour us a drink?"

Tee took two glasses from the shelf setting them on the bar, and pouring the whisky said, "Good idea."

Lifting his glass, Jim chirped, "I have some news for you."

Tee grinned, thinking he knew what was coming, "What's that?" he asked.

"Me and Maggie have decided to get married," Jim crooned.

"Well, congratulations," Tee said earnestly, lifting his glass in salute.

"I'm really glad to hear that. It makes some decisions I've been thinking about much easier for me.

"I don't hold with Texas and the South in this war so I want to go back to Illinois, and since you're getting married I'll give you my part of this store and saloon as a wedding present."

"Well, I thank you, I guess," Jim replied hesitatingly. "I hate to see you go off. I wasn't looking for that."

"I've been thinking on going back north for awhile now, and with Maggie as your partner the business will be at least as well off as you are with me. And, the truth is that I'm not giving you much of a wedding present because you know the store and saloon aren't doing very well." Tee concluded.

"You won't go before the wedding, will you?" Jim asked.

"Oh, no, I'll stay that long. When are you planning on the wedding being?"

"We thought about the first of the year."

◇

The ceremony was held in Maggie's living room on January 1, 1862 with about a dozen friends attending.

Jim walked from a side room to stand before the preacher, and stood through the ceremony without the aid of crutches.

Tee stood with Jim as his best man and thought that Maggie looked surprisingly attractive for the occasion, and was a little amused as he observed that neither of them could stop grinning.

The next morning Tee said his farewells and rode east on The Butterfield Road.

Over the next few months the business continued to decline so Jim and Maggie took the decision to change the business to a café, Maggie asserting, "There ain't been a decent café in Jacksboro since Mr. Dodson got shot."

In mid February the wood carver was set to work carving a sign for the new establishment.

"Peg-Leg Jim & Maggie's Café"

◇

Tee arrived in Cape Gerardo, Missouri in late January and immediately found work as a Chipper (Ships Carpenter's Mater) on the riverboat McCamey II, an all-wood sternwheeler plying the Mississippi, and sometimes the Ohio.

The Ships Carpenter to whom Tee was subordinate was a skilled craftsman of many years experience on riverboats, and a man Tee found agreeable to work for.

The McCamey II was old and rickety, and seemed to Tee that she wallowed along in the river currents trying her best to rattle herself to pieces. Workdays were often eighteen hours.

The food was good, most of the work wasn't disagreeable, and the boss was more than tolerable.

Soon all the river-port towns came to look so much alike Tee sometimes wondered if they had actually gone anywhere, or had they just churned around in a circle coming back where they had started.

Most of the ship's cargos were military supplies and equipment being shipped to the Quartermaster's Depot at Cairo, Illinois.

Tee knew that Charlie and Lela Haskell lived in Cairo. At least they did the last he knew. He made it a practice to stay onboard when the boat docked in Cairo.

On the one hand he longed to see Lela, on the other he was certain he didn't dare.

There were five railroads that terminated in Cairo, so it wasn't difficult for the McCamey II to pickup a load of freight to carry to Saint Louis, and in Saint Louis she would load with materials destined for Cairo.

Tee spent a little over three years nailing the McCamey II back together so she could make one more run up or down the Mississippi River.

On March 16, 1865 as the McCamey II was nearing the docks at Cairo a large sunken log became entangled in the stern-wheel ripping off paddles, twisting the metal-works of the wheel into pretzels, and damaged the drive from the wheel to the engine.

The owners decided to scrap her and all hands were let go.

◇

Rumors were flying that the war was finally coming to an end. There was great excitement, but businessmen were holding their collective breaths, not hiring, not buying, and not making any decisions.

Tee rattled around Cairo for a few days not too concerned about his situation.

According to the rumors the South was loosing the war, and Tee reasoned that if it did there would likely be great opportunities in Texas, so his plans were pending too.

One late afternoon Tee found himself walking on a street some distance from the docks that he hadn't been on before.

After a while he noticed a sign on a storefront reading, "Charlie's Ordinary."

A HANDFUL OF STARS

Knowing that an, "Ordinary," was a tavern that served food, and it being late in the day, Tee thought this could be an opportunity for some food that was different from the fare he was accustomed to.

He opened the door and stepped inside at about the same instant he realized who Charlie might be.

In the next instant the real shock hit. He recognized Lela delivering a plate of food to a man sitting at a table in the center of the room.

"Come in and have a seat Mister," she called without looking in Tee's direction. "I'll be with you in a minute."

Tee was certain he should have a seat. He wasn't certain he wasn't going to fall in the middle of the floor.

He sat transfixed as Lela floated about the room minding her chores.

She's still as beautiful as ever. Her blue eyes are still as bright, her hair still as perfect, and her figure still as trim. Look how she moves with the grace of a deer, and that mischievous little smile is still as beguiling as ever.

Oh, how I'd love to hold her.

Damnation! I wish I hadn't come in here and seen her this way.

I wonder where Charlie Haskell is? If he sees me in here he's gonna get all the wrong ideas about me being here.

Tee thought it would be a good idea to leave, but it was too late. Lela was on her way to his table.

She didn't look at him until she was handing him the menu and started to ask, as she did so, "Have something...." She stopped; her eyes went as wide as if she had seen a ghost.

She put her hand over her mouth and said almost in a whisper, "Theophilus Wells. You're the last person on earth I ever expected to see in here."

"I'm surprised to see you too. I'm sorry Lela. I didn't realize what the name on the sign implied until I saw you. I'm sorry I've intruded, I'll be going now."

"No. No, please don't. I'm very glad you've come. I just wasn't expecting to see you, that's all."

"I'd really better go. I don't expect Charlie's gonna be glad to see me."

A touch of sadness showed in her eyes for a moment when she said, "Charlie was killed over a year ago at The Battle of The Wilderness. I've just been out of mourning a little over a month."

"I'm sorry for the pain that has caused you," Tee said sincerely.

"Thank you Tee," she said softly. "I know you hated Charlie, and he hated you, but that's all in the past so let's not dwell that anymore."

Tee solemnly nodded agreement.

You weren't expecting to see me, and you didn't know Charlie was dead. Puzzled, she asked, "How did you come to be here?"

Tee explained how he had been put adrift by the wreck of the McCamey II, and how he had idly wondered into the establishment.

"So, you didn't come here looking for me?" Lela asked.

"No, I didn't, but if I'd known Charlie was dead, I would've been looking for you," Tee asserted. "You've never left my mind a day since we parted."

Her next words came softly, "Nor have you left mine." Tee thought he heard longing in her voice, he hoped he heard longing.

"I don't believe you've changed a bit in the fifteen years since we parted,' he said.

"I have changed. Maybe not much in appearance, but I was a married woman for nearly fourteen years, and I still think of myself as a married woman, and I've changed in other ways too. You may not like the person I've become."

"You're right of course. I'm just remembering your having this irritating habit of being right far too often," he said with a smile. "Neither of us are the people we each fell in love with fifteen years ago, so I suppose the thing to do is to become reacquainted with each other."

"Yes, I'd like that," she agreed.

Tee grinned, and asked, half teasing, "What do you think the odds are that your Father will shoot me before he gives me permission to see you?"

She was both amused and saddened by the question replying, "I suppose he would be kinder than he was before, but he passed away three years ago."

"I'm sorry, I didn't know," he said sincerely.

A little puzzled by her remark regarding her father's attitude, he asked, "Why do you think he would have changed his feelings toward me?"

She smiled, "The main reason he wanted me to marry Charlie is because he thought the Haskell's had money, and Father was dead broke. But, the joke was on him because the Haskell's were broke too.

"Charlie and I were barely able to scrape together enough money to buy this place."

He observed, "I seem to sense that you and Charlie were reasonably happy together."

"Yes, we were."

"Since your father isn't available, I'll ask you. Mrs. Haskell will you do me the honor of allowing me to court you?"

She sat with her back straight, her chin up, her eyes bright, and said sweetly, "Mr. Wells, I shall be delighted."

◇

That evening Tee hired a cab to drive her home. She insisted they should have walked for the distance was short.

They had little time to talk for the distance was indeed short.

Tee gave her a hand out of the cab when it stopped before the ornate Lynch Gate in front of her house. As she stepped out of the cab he took in the appearance of her house with its large windows and its gables trimmed with rococo ironwork that matched that in the gable of the gate. The yard was outlined by a white picket fence with flowerbeds along its entire length The Lynch Gate was only two feet deep, but its roof-line matched that of the house and its sides were closed by trellises where ivy grew.

Tee had the strange feeling that he would have known that this was Lela's home if he had seen it under any circumstance.

When she was out of the cab their eyes met and he realized that he still held her hand, and giving it a gentle squeeze he nodded toward her door.

Their hands and eyes broke contact when she turned to walk to her door. When they reached the door Tee tipped his hat to her and said goodnight.

◇

On April 9, 1865 Robert E. Lee surrendered thus effectively bringing the Civil War to an end. Five days later, on April 14, 1865, Abraham Lincoln was assassinated.

The effect of these events occurring with such close proximity was to put the entire country into a state of shock and confusion.

Every river-port town has more than its share of ruffians, but in the months that followed April 1865, Cairo received thousands of desperate men of every stripe. Tee took to going armed at all times and he rented a cab to drive Lela to her business each day and another to drive her home in the evening.

A HANDFUL OF STARS

The two of them had opportunities for numerous social evenings together for there was an endless string of traveling bands of entertainers making their way to Cairo.

By June 1865 Tee found himself acting as broker of goods arriving on riverboats to make their way through customs.[16] Because of the great confusion of the times, and the beginning of reconstruction efforts in the south, there were enormous opportunities for anyone with a few dollars to invest and the willingness to take some risk.

◇

On a clear Saturday afternoon in July, Tee was on his way to pick up Lela for an evening of dinner and a show when he passed a man on the street that was selling roses. He bought a dozen to take to her.

She was pleased with the gesture and expressed her pleasure by giving Tee a quick affectionate hug during which she allowed her cheek to brush his for an instant.

Tee had a very strong urge to sweep her into his arms and kiss her passionately, but he thought better of it and contented himself with the hug.

On a few other occasions he took flowers. Each time he was given a nice hug, but no kisses were forthcoming.

Times were extremely difficult for many so it wasn't unusual for men to sell their wives jewelry or anything that would bring a few dollars in order to make ends meet.

In early September a destitute man approached Tee with a necklace that he assured Tee was diamonds set in pure silver. He asked ten dollars, and insisted it was worth much more. It was pretty, but Tee didn't have any idea if it was real or not.

Tee, wanting to treat the man fairly, told him he would give him thirty percent of whatever a nearby jeweler appraised the piece to be worth.

The agreement was struck and Tee bought the necklace and had the jeweler clean it and put it in a nice box.

That gift brought a good hug and a light kiss on the lips.

Tee's mind knew better than to take advantage of the moment, but his body wanted no part of genteelness.

On the evening of September 18, Tee walked Lela to her door after an evening at a local theater where they had watched a song and dance show by a group they had never heard of.

On reaching the door he bent over and kissed her. It seemed to him an entirely natural thing to do. It wasn't much of a kiss, just an affectionate peck really.

Lela recoiled, and demanded, "Who gave you permission to take liberties with me?"

"Ah, ... Ah, I'm sor...," Tee stammered, surprised as much by his own petulance as by her reaction.

In a moment he gathered his thoughts and said, "I started to say I'm sorry, but I'm not one bit sorry. I've loved you for as long as I can remember, and I can't stand being near you like this and not having you for another minute. I want us to be together for the rest of our lives sharing all that men and women share in a lifetime.

"You chose Charlie over me before, and if you're going to reject me again I want to know now so that I can get away from you and start putting you out of my heart."

"Mr. Wells, if you wish to marry me, I'll require a proper proposal."

He swept her into his arms and kissed her passionately. She returned his kiss with equal feeling.

When the kiss had run its course they held each other. When his breath came easily enough that he could speak, he said, "I'll be here tomorrow with a ring, and a satin pillow to rest my knee upon."

A HANDFUL OF STARS

She kissed his cheek gently and whispered, "I have a satin pillow."

◇

The wedding was on October 15, 1865 in the Presbyterian Church.

In keeping with the traditions of the time that allowed only virgin brides to wear white, Lela wore a light blue gown trimmed in a slightly darker shade of blue. The gown was made in the fashion of ball gowns and was made suitable for wedding attire by having a matching jacket with long sleeves and a neckline that buttoned at her throat. The jacket bore a lace collar that matched the trim color of the gown.

The color of the gown reminded Tee of the summer sky at Clear Fork Station, with its trim matching the blue of the distant mesas.

She didn't ware a veil, but did wear a lace train matching the blue of her gown that swept around her head and draped down her back to the floor.

Lela's longtime friend Ruth was Matron of Honor and wore a gown and jacket in the same stile as Lela's gown except for being a solid color blue that matched the trim color of Lela's gown.

Tee wore a dark blue jacket over trousers that matched the blue trim of Lela's gown.

The Ships Carpenter from the McCamey II was his Best Man and wore his dress uniform.

Tee didn't know many people in Cairo, and the ones he did know also knew Lela, so the issues of who sat on which side of the church was settled by having everyone sit in the center.

They had a traditional double-ring ceremony that included brief remarks by the minister. The only words that Tee remembered was the, "love, honor, and obey," clause in her vows.

When the couple left the church those who had attended the ceremony pelted them with shoes, and there was a string of shoes tied the back of their buggy to clatter along the street behind them

After the ceremony a reception was held in the ballroom of a local hotel where food, drink, and music were provided.

The first dance was a waltz. Following it were other popular dance tunes, eventually, after sufficient lubrication, square-dance sets were called, and in the words of the next day's newspaper, "A goodtime was had by all."

The newlyweds took a honeymoon trip on a riverboat to Cincinnati where, on disembarking, an incident occurred that Lela would tease Tee about privately for the rest of his life.

Tee and Lela were approaching the gangplank to disembark when a cocky fellow passenger smirked, because they hadn't been out of their cabin the entire journey, "Have a good trip?"

Tee turned and in the same motion knocked the man over the rail into the water. He then stepped to the rail and called to the man, "Had a damned site better trip than you did."

◇

On their return to Cairo they settled into a routine of tending their businesses, participating in civic organizations, and dabbling in local politics in supportive roles, not as candidates for office.

They became a happily married middle-aged couple working to make their fortune.

◇

CHAPTER 6

A Handful Of Stars

March 10, 1868 a letter from Jim.

Dear Brother,
Hope this finds you and Lela enjoying good health and doing well in your businesses.

Maggie and I are both well, and have great hopes for our future fortunes in a new town just being built about three miles down the river from our old Clear Fork Station store and saloon.

The Federals have established a new line of forts along the frontier to protect the settlers who are moving into this country, and new towns are springing up near most of them.

Maggie and I have decided to move our café to the afore mentioned place at the foot of Government Hill where upon stands the newly established Fort Griffin.[17]

There is great opportunity for any kind of business a man wants to put in here for people of all kinds are pouring in.

There are plenty of rowdy toughs, gamblers, and sporting women, (some are calling the sporting district Notchville).

There are also lots of good folks who want to settle the country and raise good kids, good crops, and cattle. Many of the settlers we knew before the war are still in this country and doing their best to make a good place of it.

Maggie and me would love for you and Lela to come out here and join us in helping build a new town in a place where there hasn't been anything before.

If you have any thought of returning to Texas I believe this is the place to be.

If you don't want to come and stay, we'd be pleased to have you come for a visit.

We look forward to hearing from you soon.

We do hope you will at least come for a visit.

Your Brother,
Jim Wells

While Tee and Lela sat in their living room before dinner that evening he read the letter aloud to her.

When he finished reading he looked up from the paper and commented, "Those Texans. Notchville. I declare they do have a talent for naming things. If you ever see that Clear Fork River you'll know exactly what I mean."

Tee and Lela had never discussed the possibility of moving to Texas. It hadn't occurred to her that he might want to return there.

"Do you want to go back to Texas?" She asked.

"Not now. Our businesses are doing well here. Why would we want to move?"

She looked relieved.

He went on, "If business turns sour here Texas is a possibility we might consider."

"Would you like to go for a visit?" she inquired.

"Sure. Sometime"

"We haven't been on a trip since our honeymoon, so why don't we plan a trip out there this year?"

He was taken a little by surprise, "You'd really like to do that?"

"Yes. Wouldn't you?"

"Yeah, I'll write Jim a letter tomorrow and let him know we'll be coming out. Just for a visit, right?"

"If you say so," she assented.

◇

Tee and Lela booked passage on a riverboat traveling down the Mississippi River to Simmesport, Louisiana. There they changed to a smaller boat to travel up the Red River coming eventually to Jefferson, Texas.

In Jefferson Tee bought a horse and buggy and outfitted with camping gear.

Leaving Jefferson early in the morning of September 12, 1868 the couple wandered through the East Texas piney woods paralleling the westward course of the Red River.

Late in the afternoon of their first day on the trail, Tee stopped the buggy in a small clearing adjacent to a clear flowing creek and announced that they would camp here for the night.

Lela climbed out of the buggy, stretched her tired muscles, and said demurely, "I must tend my private needs."

Understanding her meaning, Tee replied, pointing to a nearby shrub, "I thought I would go behind that bush over there."

Seeing no alternative, Lela stalked off into the bushes.

When she returned in a few minutes she saw that Tee had gathered wood for a fire and had laid their bedding on the ground near the buggy.

"Where's the tent?" she inquired.

"I didn't buy a tent."

"Why on earth not?"

"Sleeping in a tent is likely to give you a fever."

Becoming a little impatient, "Where did you get that notion?"

"From reading The Prairie Traveler[18]. In his book Marcy describes a study done by the French and the American Armies of men sleeping in tents and men sleeping in the open, and they found that the men who slept in tents were four times as likely to come down with fevers as the men who slept in the open.

"Marcy says he thinks the fevers seep up out of the ground and are trapped in the tent thus affecting the men."

Placing her hands on her hips, and pitching her voice in an assertive tone, Lela stated, "Theophilus Wells I am not a solder, and this is not a prairie, it's a forest. If you expect me to camp you buy a tent, and while you're about it buy a chamber pot too. I don't intend to conduct my privet business squatting in the woods like a squaw."

◇

On their fifth day out of Jefferson they arrived in Denison, Texas, where they hit the Old Butterfield Road.

After four more days on the trail, they finally came to The Flats below Fort Griffin.

Driving along Griffin Avenue they encountered a man who was about to walk across the street before whom Tee stopped the horse and inquired of the man, "Can you tell me how to find the home of Jim and Maggie Wells/"

The man was not quite medium height, slender, well dressed, and clean-shaven.

He gave Tee an appraising look and said politely, "I haven't seen you here before."

Understanding the remark to be a question, he replied, "I'm Jim's brother, Tee," nodding at Lela, "and this is my wife Lela."

The man tipped his hat to Lela and extended his hand to Tee saying, "I'm John Larn[19]. Your brother's house is two streets over, the second house on the left."

"I'm pleased to make your acquaintance Mr. Larn, and thank you for your help."

"Likewise, and a good day to you," Larn replied and motioned for Tee to drive ahead.

"And to you sir," Tee replied as he put the horse into motion.

When they were out of earshot of Mr. Larn, Lela said, "I'm a little surprised to meet a gentleman like that here. I wasn't expecting anything but ruffians and outlaws here."

"Yes, he seemed a pleasant enough gent didn't he," Tee observed.

◇

After dinner that evening, Tee and Jim adjourned to the front porch leaving the house to the two women.

Having taken a jug and their smoking materials with them they made themselves comfortable in a couple of high-backed cane-bottomed rocking chairs.

When they had each had a draw on the jug, and had a smoke going, Tee remarked, "This sure is a lot different country than it was when we first came out here back in fifty-eight (1858)."

"Yeah, it sure is," Jim, agreed.

"It would have been nice to have been in a town instead of out in the middle of nowhere the way we were at Clear Fork Station."

Jim drew on his pipe and made no answer.

"You ever go back out there?" Tee inquired.

"No, I haven't."

"I'm thinking that I will drive Lela up there tomorrow to show her the old place. Be glad for you and Maggie to come with us. We'll make a day of it."

"I thank you brother, but I reckon not. I don't do well in open country on this peg-leg, and we need to stay here and tend the café.

"But, you folks go right ahead, we'll be here when you get back."

Each man took a turn with the jug and drew slowly on their smokes while watching the red afterglow of a clear sunset.

After a long silence Tee commented, "I reckon a man wouldn't have to wait three days for his first customer to show up if he opened a saloon in this town the way we did at Clear Fork Station."

Jim chuckled, "No, I don't expect he would."

"Old Howdy Jones," Tee mused. "He was a likable cuss. I sure hate the way he turned out."

"Yeah, that was mighty sorry alright. I always liked Old Howdy myself," Jim admitted.

"I don't suppose you ever hear anything of him anymore? Tee asked.

"Oh," Jim started in a subdued tone, "about two months after you went to Missouri Howdy came back to visit Roseanne.

"They caught him and tried him for rustling and sentenced him to twenty years. But the judge told him if he would join the army and serve honorably that he would put him on probation when he came back.

"So, Howdy took him up on that offer, but he would have done better to have gone to the pen. He was killed when the Damned Yankees blew up the works at Petersburg."

"I hate to hear that," Tee offered. "Some say an honorable death is the better way to go."

"The only ones who say that is old men that send the young ones off to do the fighting," Jim observed.

A HANDFUL OF STARS

Each man took a turn with the jug and smoked in silence while staring into the dying embers of the sunset for a short time before Tee inquired, "What's become of Colonel Smith?"

"Well, he went to New Mexico with General Sibley[20] and John Baylor when they tried to take over the territory. They declared Baylor the governor and that New Mexico was a Confederate State," Jim started.

"That the same Baylor that tried to mob the Indians about the time we came out here?" Tee interrupted.

"That's the one," Jim assured. "It didn't take them Damned Yankees from Santa Fe and Colorado long to kick the stuffing's out of them Texas boys at Glorieta Pass[21*] and send the whole delegation back home with their tails between their legs.

"Colonel Smith took a mini ball in his shoulder that festered up on him and he died two days after he got home."

Tee took a draw on his smoke, and blowing the smoke out said, "I never did like that man much, but I didn't wish him dead. He did his best for Texas and I guess he did what he thought was right in whatever he was involved in."

"He was one of them old-time mossbacks alright," Jim agreed.

The sun was completely gone now, and there were millions of stars visible in the clear night sky. The brothers sat drawing on their smokes and sharing an occasional sip on the jug.

"Are there any of the other folks we knew from the old days still around this country?" Tee probed.

"Once in a while I see someone from back then, but I don't really know how many are still around this country. There's other towns sprung up where they can do business, and these here Flats are so rowdy that decent folks try to stay away as much as they can.

"I did see that fellow that his wife was scalped, I can't remember his name, a few days ago."

"His name is Ward Phillips," Tee recalled.

"He's still farming down the river someplace," Jim went on. "But I heard that his wife went kinda crazy after she was scalped and has gone back East somewhere."

Jim knocked the cold ashes out of his pipe, and continued, "Phillips went to Bandera and got his boy you took over there, but them Miller boys went off searching for the woman and boy them Indians took and never went and got the girl."

"That's been nine years ago. I reckon them tads would be near grown now," Tee observed.

"Well, it's a pity what's happened to the Indians in this country, but they sure don't do anything to help their own cause. I expect if them Miller boys found that woman and boy after all these years they'd be real disappointed in what they found," Jim asserted.

"I expect you're right about that," Tee agreed.

The brothers sat in silence, each lost in their own thoughts, observing the darkening night. They took an occasional sip from the jug, and remained silent.

◇

At midmorning Tee and Lela drove north along Griffin Avenue. Lela turned her gaze upstream of the river thereby ignoring the row of prostitute's cribs that lined River Road adjacent to the river.

After fording the river they took the Fort Richardson Road to its intersection with the Old Butterfield Road where they turned west toward Clear Fork Station.

That portion of the Old Butterfield Road having been lightly used since the stagecoaches had stopped using it was somewhat overgrown, but with some maneuvering it was entirely passable.

A HANDFUL OF STARS

Eventually the old road crested at the edge of the river's valley where Tee expected to be able to see the buildings that he and Jim had built for Clear Fork Station. From the ridge he couldn't see anything he remembered.

He drove on into the river valley and approached the old river ford near the place where he expected to see the store and saloon building. He was at first confused; seeing nothing he thought he had taken a wrong turn somewhere.

After a brief survey of the site, he spotted the corral fence that he and Jim had built when they first arrived here. It was overgrown with weeds and thorny cactus and briers.

Stepping out of the buggy, and offering a hand to Lela, he announced, "This is where it was."

"Here?" Sounding disappointed, she went on, "There's nothing here, I expected to see the store and saloon you've talked about so much."

"It was here. I suppose the settlers in the area must have taken the stone for their own purposes."

They walked the area and Tee pointed out where the store and saloon had stood, where the stagecoaches had stopped to change their teams, and where the feed shed had been.

Drawing Lela's attention to a scrubby mesquite bush that grew in the bend of a dry-wash about sixty yards away, Tee said, "Over there near that bush is the place where I shot Thad Simpson."

"You've told me about that, and you still have nightmares about it sometimes too," she said sympathetically.

"I do still dream about shooting that man sometimes," Tee said, speaking as much to himself as to Lela. "I don't dream about shooting the Indian boy at Tarpley Pass or Thad's brother John, who shot Jim's leg off, but I can still see the look in Thad's eyes knowing that he's been killed, and damning me to hell for the doing of it."

Lela squeezed his hand gently, but made no comment.

They wandered around the area coming eventually to where the corral gate had stood.

Tee slipped his arm around her and said, "One cool clear night a long time ago I stood in this very spot looking at the stars. They looked so close that I thought I would like to reach up there and pick a handful and sprinkle them in your hair."

"Did you?" she asked smiling.

"Yes, I did. But I can see standing here now, with the sun gleaming in your hair, and the sparkle in your eyes, that all the stars in heaven wouldn't add a whit to your beauty nor to my adoration of you."

Kissing him sweetly, she whispered, "Thank you, Tee. That's a very sweet thing for you to say to me."

After a moment she turned to walk to the buggy and having taken a step she clutched his arm saying, "I'm a little dizzy. Let me hold your arm back to the buggy."

He swept her off her feet and carried her to the buggy.

Making her comfortable in the buggy, he asked, "Are you going to be alright?"

Tee was confused by the impish little girl look Lela gave him, but his confusion was soon allayed by the feigned innocence in her answer. "Oh yes, I'm going to be fine in about seven months, right after the stork pays us a visit."

EPILOGUE

The ladies who attend the Creative Writing Circle at The Heritage Senior Center in Irving, Texas unanimously objected to the end of "A Handful Of Stars."

So, for the ladies:

◇

Tee and Lela returned to Cairo, Illinois where on February 14, 1869 the stork delivered Ester.

◇

Twenty-five years later Ester, her two young sons, and her husband were traveling through Texas by train while on their way to California.

When the train they were riding in was huffing its way up the Baird Escarpment a few miles east of Abilene, Texas, Ester remarked to her boys, "Grandpa Tee and Uncle Jim use to run a stagecoach station a few miles north of here."

"Yeah," the older boy cried. "And Grandpa shot two bad men and an Indian."

"And one of the bad men shot Uncle Jim's leg off," the younger boy confided.

The older boy turned to his brother pointing his finger in pretext of a pistol shouting, "Play like I'm Grandpa and you're the Indian. Bang, bang, bang."

The younger boy crumpled to the floor clutching his chest only to spring up instantly pointing his finger and calling, "Play like I'm Grandpa and you're the bad man. Bang, bang, bang."

BIBLIOGRAPHICAL NOTE

While researching and writing this novel, the author gratefully acknowledges valuable insights and information gained from reading the following works.

Bearss, Edwin C. and Gibson, Arrell M. *Fort Smith Little Gibraltar on the Arkansas* (1969)

Clayton, Lawrence and Farmer, Joan Holford editors. *Tracks Along the Clear Fork* (2000)

Crawford, Max. *Lords of the Plain* (1997)

DeArment, Robert K. *Bravo of the Brazos* (2002)

Fay, Ted. *The Twenty Mule Team of Death Valle* (DVD 2006)

Green, A. C. *900 Miles on The Butterfield Trail* (1994)

Marcy, Randolph B. *The Prairie Traveler* (1859)

Ornsby, Waterman L. *The Butterfield Overland Mail* (1859) edited by Lyle H. Wright and Josephine M. Bynum (1955)

Reynolds Matthews, Sally *Interwoven* (1936)

Shelton, Gene. *Brazos Dreamer* (1993)

Wilbarger, John Wesley, *Indian Depredations In Texas* (1985)

FOOTNOTES

¹ #3 tub: A #3 tub is three feet in diameter and eighteen inches deep. Usually made of galvanized steel or wood.

²* Lucifer: An obsolete term for a strike anywhere kitchen size wooden match.

³ John Warren Butterfield (1801 – 1869) Born near Berne, New York, he became a professional stagecoach driver at age 19. He later founded companies that became American Express and Wells Fargo. In 1857 he founded the Butterfield Overland Mail and operated a stagecoach line carrying mail between St Louis and San Francisco from 1858 to 1861.

⁴ The Near Wheel Mule: The mule nearest the left front wheel of the wagon.

⁵* Jerk-Line: A single rein attached to the lead mule on the left side of the team. The mule was trained to respond to a steady pull on the jerk-line by turning left thus causing the whole team to turn left while a series of pulls, or jerks, caused the mule to turn right thus turning the team right.

⁶ Camp Cooper: Established May 1856 about seven miles upstream of Clear Fork Station. Was surrendered to Texas Militia in February 1861 when Texas seceded from the Union.

⁷ Old Camp Cooper: Camp Cooper was temporarily moved to another location, then returned to its original location and thereafter referred to as Old Camp Cooper.

⁸ Celerity Coach: The Celerity Coach was sometimes referred to as a mud wagon because of its lightweight construction and four inch wide steel tiers. It was equipped with three bench-seats that were designed to lay flat so that the passengers could lie down to sleep. The wagon was covered with a canvas top mounted on bows and had curtains that could be closed in inclement weather. Celerity Coaches were used on the mail run between Fort Smith and San Francisco.

⁹* Waterman L. Ormsby's articles were published in a series of six articles in the New York Herald from September 26, 1858 to November 19, 1858. Mr. Ormsby was the only through passenger on the first westbound run of The Butterfield Overland Mail.

¹⁰ John Robert Baylor (July 27, 1822-February 8, 1894) served as a Judge, State Legislator, rancher, prospector, and Indian Agent, in Texas, and as Military Governor of New Mexico Territory, and an officer in the Confederate States Army

¹¹ Major Robert S. Neighbors (Nov. 3, 1815-Sep.14, 1859) Major in the Army of The Republic of Texas, Assisted Captain Randolph Marcy with the survey of the San Antonia—El Pasco High Road, served as Indian Agent for The Republic of Texas,

served as State Legislator, was instrumental in establishing the reservation system in Texas. Served terms as Indian Agent under two U. S. Presidents. Was instrumental in the removal of John Baylor as Indian Agent in Texas.

[12] St. Theophilus: Saint Theophilus the Penitent or Theophilus of Adana (died in 538) became bishop of Adana (now part of Turkey). According to legend, he became bishop by making a deal with the Devil. Later regretting his deal, he repented, fasted, and prayed until he was forgiven. The Devil didn't release him from their contract until he received forgiveness from the man he had wronged.

[13] Major Robert S. Neighbors was gunned down on the street of the village of Belknap on September 14, 1859 while on his way home to Austin from having escorted the Indians from the Clear Fork reservations to their new home at Fort Sill.

[14] Divisions on the Route: 6th Division-Fort Chadbourne 55 miles north of present day San Angelo, Texas, to Colbert's Ferry on the Red River north of the present day town of Sherman, Texas.

[15] Fort Davis: Not to be confused with the military installation of the same name in Jeff Davis County Texas. This Fort Davis was in Stephens County Texas on the banks of the Clear Fork of the Brazos River and was a civilian fortified community that was abandoned by its inhabitance shortly after the Civil War ended.

[16] Cairo, Illinois Custom House: Cairo become an important transportation center and was an inland port of entry. The Old Customhouse is now a museum and library and is listed in the National Register of Historic Places

[17] Fort Griffin: July 1867-May 1882. The town of Fort Griffin, or The Flats, became one of the most notorious, "wide open," western frontier towns of the 1870s. Now a State Historic Site about 40 miles northeast of Abilene, Texas.

[18] The Prairie Traveler by Captain Randolph B. Marcy was first published in 1859. It soon became the principal manual for the westward-bound pioneers.

[19] John Larn: Notorious killer, cattle rustler, and horse thief. Served one term as sheriff of Shackelford County beginning in May 1876 with his best friend John Selman, who later murdered John Wesley Harden, as his chief deputy. While sheriff Larn was the leader of the vigilante Tin Hat-Band Brigade. Members of the Tin Hats killed Larn while he lay shackled in the old log jail in Albany, Texas on June 24, 1878 having become fearful that Larn was about to turn states evidence against them.

[20] Henry Hopkins Sibley (May 25, 1816 – August 23, 1886) was a brigadier general during the American Civil War fighting in the Confederate States Army in the New Mexico Territory.

[21*] The Battle of Glorieta Pass (near Santa Fe, New Mexico) took place on March 26-28, 1862.